UNDINE

UNDINE

PENNI RUSSON

GREENWILLOW BOOKS
An Imprint of HarperCollins Publishers

Undine
Copyright © 2004 by Penni Russon
First published in 2004 in Australia
by Random House Australia.
First published in 2006 in the United States
by Greenwillow Books.

The text of this book is set in Adobe Caslon.
Book design and photography by Chad W. Beckerman.

Library of Congress Cataloging-in-Publication Data
Russon, Penni.
Undine / by Penni Russon.
p. cm.
"Greenwillow Books."
Summary: Sixteen-year-old Undine, hearing her presumably deceased father calling to her and feeling a strange force growing inside her, travels to the sea to discover the depths of her magical powers.
ISBN 0-06-079389-9 (trade).
ISBN 0-06-079390-2 (lib. bdg.)
[1. Magic—Fiction. 2. Fathers and daughters—Fiction. 3. Ocean—Fiction. 4. Conduct of life—Fiction. 5. Interpersonal relations—Fiction. 6. Australia—Fiction.] I. Title.
PZ7.R9194U64 2006 [Fic]—dc22 2004059757

First American Edition 10 9 8 7 6 5 4 3 2 1

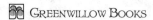 GREENWILLOW BOOKS

FOR
MARTIN & FRÉDÉRIQUE
WITH LOVE

PROLOGUE

Underneath the sound of the sea, the regular sigh of waves advancing and withdrawing, *she* is there.

He waits. It seems he has always been waiting, with infinite patience, on an endless beach.

If you put your ear to his temple or his chest you would hear the sea. It tires him, the waves beating relentlessly against him. He used to dream of *dry*: deserts, mountains, canyons made of hard, split rock, *heart*lands, where the sea never intrudes. *Now would I give a thousand furlongs of sea for an acre of barren ground—long heath, brown furze, anything.*

But today he dreams of a girl. She moves in the air around him.

He has been waiting for years—since he first conceived the idea of her, even before the first cell split, and she began to take hold on the world. She is coming. She will wear the ocean wrapped around her. She will bring a new sky.

There is a map inside her, as real and belonging as much to her body as the fine network of veins on her pale wrists; a map she has always carried, and it is of this place. The journey begins inland—in a house, in a room—and spirals outward. The journey begins in a mirror.

She will come. It will be over. It will have begun.

Part One

CHAPTER ONE

Undine trailed down the stairs to the bathroom. She felt a lump of something, starting at the base of her spine and working its way upward. It wasn't a physical something, though it belonged inside her body, under her skin, trapped inside the fine network of muscle, tissue, nerves, and bone. She knew what was happening because it had happened before and even though she felt a shiver of fear, she told herself firmly that mostly she was annoyed, because it was Tuesday, and Tuesdays were—on the whole—not to be trusted.

As the lump worked its way up and prepared to inhabit her mind, she spoke sharply to it. "Stop it. Stop it. Not on *Tuesdays*."

It stopped for the time being, and she managed to continue her preparations for the day: locating her math book, extricating her homework from Jasper's tight grasp—"Mine, mine," said Jasper, and, You can have it, thought Undine. But she continued to prise Jasper's fingers away and replaced the assignment with a bank statement so Jasper wouldn't cry. She dressed herself in her crumpled uniform and settled on one blue sock and one almost-blue sock because, after all, it was Tuesday and not everything could be expected to go right.

Tuesdays were just badly designed, she thought crossly, as Lou danced in front of her with a piece of burnt toast and a coffee. They didn't have the anticipation and freshness of Mondays, when you woke up with the weekend still singing in your mind, and made resolutions to be more organized for the rest of the week, and looked forward to school so you could hear who wore what to Nick's party and the various assorted minutiae that colored other people's lives. By Tuesday, the weekend was well and truly done with—old news—and the next weekend felt a long way away.

Undine ate a halfhearted breakfast while Lou tried to pack Jasper's backpack with the absurd quantity of stuff an almost-three-year-old was expected to take to day care. Jasper was sitting at his table and chair set, made of bright yellow plastic, conducting experiments with his toast and juice. Undine eyed the results queasily, her own toast flipping over in her stomach, and decided it was a good time to beat a hasty retreat.

She swept on Lou in midflight to give her a kiss good-bye, and—remembering the feeling she had had that morning—an oversized hug. Lou raised her eyebrows.

"Tuesdays aren't *that* bad, Undine. I'm sure we'll both survive another one. Off you go, horrible adolescent, or you'll miss the bus."

Undine shrugged and smiled foolishly, but the

shiver of fear returned. She bent down and buried her face in Jasper's hair, which smelled of vegemite and orange juice. Jasper was busy squelching wet toast through his fingers. Undine sighed.

"How about *you* be the horrible adolescent and I'll be the baby."

Jasper gave her a withering look. "I'm not a baby. I'm a Busy Bee," he said, naming the big kids' room at day care that he had graduated into early because he was too boisterous for the toddlers' room.

"Too busy for me," said Undine cheerfully, surveying the results of his industry and giving him another squeeze.

"Go on," said Lou, shooing Undine away with both arms, "before I make you clean up this child."

Undine ran through the door, shaking off the residual feelings and flutters of fear, determined to push them way, way down for as long as she could. Still, she couldn't help but peek back through the living room window, to see Jasper patting his juice and toast concoction onto Lou's smiling face.

• • •

Undine lived in the old part of Hobart near the rivulet, in a crooked little house that was halfway up a concrete flight of stairs between two streets.

It was a very complicated place to live, because the two streets were in different suburbs and controlled by different councils, and no one could ever decide exactly which street they lived on. Their mail came addressed to either 2½ Myrtle Street (which was below them), or 43b Camelot Road (which was above them). Every year arrangements were made about the rates, but the next year they would receive two bills and the councils would bicker over it, with Lou caught in the middle.

Every time the bills arrived, Lou would sigh and say, "I wish, just once, neither of them would send us a bill."

Although the house was a bit dilapidated, its thick stone had been covered with whitewashed stucco, and it had a pale blue door and shutters on the front window. The house looked as if it belonged more in the glaring whitish-blue light of the Greek islands than under Australian pepperminty gums scribbling their branches in the sky overhead.

There was a long, crouching attic bedroom at the top of the house for Undine, a bigger bedroom downstairs for Lou, and a triangle-shaped space that jutted out unexpectedly to one side of the house for Jasper.

Most of the time Undine liked living in No-Man's-Land, as she and her mother called it. She loved her bedroom, with its sloped ceiling and long windows on either side, looking over the back garden at one end and the steps at the other. The window that looked over the front was what Lou called a French window, which meant it was big enough to climb out of, onto a balcony that was just the right size for her to sit on. She had put up shelves on the outside walls and crowded them with busy little pots of geraniums. It was her favorite place to be; she felt like Rapunzel or Juliet, or some other fated and mysterious woman, sitting up there, watching the sky for bats on the edge of dusk, or eating bread and honey on a summer Sunday morning.

Undine flung herself down the steps, which were too long to walk down and just the right length for running, though you tended to gather an unnerving momentum on the way. She knocked on the side door of 2 Myrtle Street, not waiting for an answer before letting herself in. Number two had a grand front entrance, with a small avenue of trees that made Undine feel like a princess when she walked beneath the arching branches. It was a bit overwhelming, however, to feel like a princess every day, so most days she came in this side door, which was just the right size for her, though most people had to duck their heads. The Montmorencys referred to it as the servants' entrance, and Undine found it far more relaxing to be a goose girl or a handmaiden than a princess, especially when she was wearing a rather too-small school uniform and mismatched socks.

Mrs. M eyed her with the same mixture of friendliness and suspicion with which she always regarded Undine. As the mother of boys, she had never quite forgiven Undine for transforming from an angular, boyish child into a surprisingly shapely teenager.

"Hi, Mrs. M." Undine grinned. "Is Trout ready to go?"

"He's in his room," Mrs. M said, disapprovingly. Undine smiled and gave Mrs. M a funny little salute, touching her forehead and flicking her fingers away, before running up the stairs to Trout's room.

"I don't know why she can't just wait down here," Mrs. M grumbled to her husband. "Make conversation with us, like normal people."

Mr. M scuffled through the papers. "Leave her alone," he said good-naturedly. "She's hardly a sex kitten. Besides, with our three boys, I think her mother has more right to worry than you do."

Mrs. M looked disgusted. "Sex kitten! Really, Patrick. Our boys," she went on, without conviction, "are sweet, innocent and unworldly. They're not ready for that much leg."

"Richard is nineteen. Dan is eighteen. And Trout and Undine are sixteen. You've got to let it happen sometime. Anyway, Trout isn't interested in girls. He's got too much *thinking* to do to notice anyone's legs. I wouldn't mind if he did look at a few legs. It isn't healthy to read as much as that boy does."

Trout looked up as Undine entered the room. His father would have been pleased to know that Trout did notice Undine's legs, and a lot more besides. But they had been friends for years, and Trout had no experience in affairs of the heart, particularly not for so complex a task as negotiating their comfortable friendship into something more *dire*, more passionate and unwieldy. Besides, Trout was fairly sure Undine never noticed his legs and he would have been ashamed if she had. They were knobbly and lumpy and looked more like they belonged to a ten-year-old than to someone "on the threshold of adulthood" (their school principal's term).

All in all, Trout thought unhappily as Undine

flung herself onto his bed, she takes me for granted. She trusts me too much, and girls never feel passionate about boys they trust.

"Come on," Undine said, "we're going to be late for school."

"Oh, *school*," said Trout derisively, but they both knew he rather liked school, the learning part of it anyway. He closed the book he had been reading with a loud thump—all the books Trout read were thumpers—and picked up his schoolbag. Undine stood up next to him as he looked at himself in the mirror, and for a moment they were framed together, just the way he wanted.

At least he was taller than her, he thought ruefully, though that wasn't hard as Undine was what his mother politely called "diminutive in stature." She had wild hair, at present dyed red, which kind of frizzed out in all directions. She had a nice body too, and something Trout knew, but had never told Undine, was that she was often discussed in the boys' locker room. Funnily enough, no one ever really asked her out. She was possibly *too* sexy for the average ego of a teenage boy. She was also too smart for most high school boys, and despite their big talk he knew many of the boys were a little afraid of her. Even if she said yes to one of them, they wouldn't know what to do with her once they had her alone. But Trout loved her brain just as much as the rest of her. He sighed, and the Trout in the mirror sighed back. Her reflected self looked at him, and he shook himself out of it.

"Well, come on then, fellow scholar," he said. "Let us go anon to that place of information and bookishness."

Undine's reflection drooped and for a moment he saw a flicker of worry play across her slight features.

"Something up?" He tried to sound genuinely concerned while holding back the very real tenderness that threatened to take over his voice. He wasn't sure if he had succeeded.

"I . . ." Undine faltered. "No. Just ordinary Tuesday blues."

But she leaned over a little and kind of nudged him affectionately with her arm. Something stirred in him. Oh that old thing, he thought, and he left with Undine for school, dragging his longing behind him.

The feeling that Undine had been trying to submerge since she woke up had returned in Trout's bedroom. She had seen something in her own face that hadn't been there yesterday. She looked *older*, or more world-weary maybe. But it was an expression that didn't entirely belong to her, as if the film of someone else's face had been projected onto her features.

And then there was the way Trout had looked at her. She had suspected for some time that he had *feelings* for her, messy, perilous feelings, and she didn't like to think about it. She preferred friendship to sex—or to the idea of sex anyway, having no practical experience to draw on. Usually she jollied Trout out of it whenever he started looking moonish and longing. But today she simply felt as if she couldn't bear it, not on top of that other thing.

She sat silently next to Trout on the way to school, waves of dread building inside her. She had tried her best to ignore the feeling fizzing through her bones, sitting in the center of her stomach. But by the time the bus pulled in to the driveway at school, Trout had lapsed into an uneasy silence as well, disconcerted by her lack of responsiveness.

They had started walking toward the main building when Undine suddenly stopped.

"What's wrong?" Trout asked, and she could hear that wobble in his voice, the one she dreaded: tenderness, awkward desire.

She reached into her bag and pulled out her math homework, shoving it into Trout's hand.

"Here," she said. "Give this to Mr. Anderson. I don't think I can face school today."

"You and your Tuesdays! You can't just leave."

"Can't I?" And Undine walked back up the

driveway, and out of the school grounds. She didn't have to turn around to know Trout was still there, watching her walk away. She didn't look back. She just kept walking.

CHAPTER TWO

She was still walking an hour later, off the main road and into the meandering backstreets. She didn't really know where she was going, though she seemed to be heading toward home. Home wasn't a great idea, because Lou was a book indexer and she worked at home. In a matter such as this, Lou was unpredictable. She could well take one look at Undine and send her to bed until she felt ready to face the world again. Or she could pack Undine into the car, feeling or no feeling, drive her back to school, and walk her to class to make sure she went in.

Undine veered off to the left, with no destination in mind. She needed to know exactly what it was the feeling signified, but she had no idea how to even begin finding that out. "What's the *point* of you," Undine grumbled, "if I don't know what you mean?"

The last time she had felt like this was almost four years ago. Lou had been pregnant with Jasper. Undine had tried to tell Lou about her feeling, but Lou had waved it away. "Growing pains," she called it. Undine had carried it around with her for a week, this growing awful anxiety. Her heart would start racing for no real reason, and she'd feel a little panicky flutter, as though something terrible was about to happen and she could do nothing. She hung around the house, watching Lou like a hawk, because she thought it meant something was going to happen to the baby.

Then the police came to the door, a man and a

woman. They were hot and flustered. They'd had trouble finding the place, and Undine heard Lou explaining to them about 2½ Myrtle Street and 43b Camelot Road. The man just stood there, uncomfortable, looking all starched and stiff in his uniform. The woman smiled softly at Lou, a silencing kind of smile. Undine slipped up next to Lou, and Lou's hand blindly searched out her own.

Stephen had been in a car accident on his way home from work. Just before the policeman told them this, Undine saw, as though it were printed on the air in front of her, the moving image of Stephen's little red car being hit by a bigger car, and Stephen's calm face as he lost control of the car and was spun into one of those big concrete pylons at the bridge's exit. Undine's heart stopped racing for the first time in days, and then seemed to stop altogether. The floor rushed up to meet her, but then she realized it was her falling to meet the floor. The policewoman stepped in and caught her, just before she hit the ground, and carried her over to the couch, clutching too hard under her arms so she pinched the skin. Undine felt raw under there for days. The police stayed for a minute or two, their soft babbling voices caressing the air around Undine's head, and then Undine seemed to drift off, because when she looked up they had gone. Lou was standing at the open door, staring into space.

"I thought they were here about the parking tickets," Lou said as she closed the door, and then she burst into terrifying tears.

The dreadful immediacy of Undine's feeling had dissolved then, to be replaced by the numbness of grief, and, horribly, a sense of relief, that the *thing* had just happened and there was nothing she could have done to prevent it. With the relief came guilt, and that guilt was pushed right down inside her, becoming so tangled up in her feelings about Stephen that after a while she came to believe that she was somehow responsible for his death. It was her worst and most secret thought; it was the thought she used to torture herself whenever she felt she had behaved badly and needed to punish herself, like when she picked on Jasper or was mean to Lou.

Sometimes over the days after Stephen died, Undine had caught Lou *studying* her, examining her face as if she were written in a foreign language. Undine didn't mention her feelings to Lou, or to anyone. That expression on Lou's face had made Undine feel like a stranger.

Stephen was Jasper's father, but he was not Undine's, though in a way he belonged more to Undine than Jasper, because Undine had known him and loved him and Jasper had not. Stephen had fallen in love with Lou when Undine was ten and together they had moved into the house on the steps. They'd only had him three years when he died, but Lou and Undine found they had to learn all over again how to be a family without him.

Undine turned another corner and found herself on Mim's street. Mim was her "aunt," Stephen's sister.

Undine stood outside Mim's redbrick house, wondering whether or not to go inside. An enormous brown cat, moving like a puppet on strings, made his way slowly and sleepily toward her, leaping surprisingly lightly onto the gatepost.

"Hello, Lizard." Undine scooped him up and buried her nose in the fur on his neck. Lizard had once been hers, from when he was a kitten and they lived in the little flat in Bellerive. When Jasper was born, Lou had wanted to give Lizard away, leading to fights and recriminations and some pretty dedicated sulking on Undine's part. Mim, to end the argument, had agreed to "borrow" him until Jasper was older.

Undine listened to the internal rumbling of the cat's purr. It was like a hidden mechanism, a little machine pumping inside him.

"Undine!"

Mim was coming around the house from the back garden, wiping dirt onto the front of her baggy shirt.

"I wondered what made old Boof take off so fast. Usually you can't get him to move without a food-based incentive. That cat has a sixth sense when it comes to you."

Undine's smile was almost a scowl. She didn't want to think about extra senses at that moment.

Mim cocked her head and looked circumspectly at Undine. She must have realized that it was a school day. She leaned against the fence and began digging through the many pockets of her green pants for cigarettes.

"You know," she said, between her teeth as she lit up, "if you're going to wag school, you should really take a change of clothes with you."

Undine looked down at her school uniform. "It wasn't exactly planned."

"Something up, mate? You're not in trouble, are you?"

Undine shook her head, not looking terribly sure. "Not as far as I know."

"Come on," said Mim. "Let's grab a cuppa and you can tell me what's going on."

• • •

One of the best things about Stephen was the instant family he had brought into Undine's and Lou's lives. It had always been just Lou and Undine. Suddenly, as well as Stephen, there were grandparents, aunts, an uncle, and cousins.

Mim was extraspecial though. She was still in her twenties, quite young for an aunt. She had loved Undine and Lou, and they had loved her, from the moment they met. She was different from everyone Undine knew. She was too young to be a mum, so she never tried to mother Undine. She was surer of herself than the girls Undine knew at school, even though her hair was always in a messy ponytail, and most of her wardrobe consisted of secondhand men's clothing. But she had what Undine supposed was *style* and looked sexier in them than any of the girls at school ever did in their itsy skirts and little huggy T-shirts.

"Okay, you," Mim said, putting a coffee in her hands. "What's the story?"

They were sitting on Mim's back veranda, looking out over the garden. It was enormous, with what looked like hundreds of different kinds of plants vying for space. Undine fiddled with a frond of jasmine spilling over the edge of the veranda.

"It's . . ." Undine didn't know where to begin. "It's kind of hard to explain."

"Try me."

Undine looked at Mim over the top of her coffee cup. "You'll think I'm crazy."

"I know you're crazy. Come on. You'll probably feel better if you tell me."

"It's this . . . I've been having . . . feelings. A feeling. Since I woke up this morning."

Mim smiled blankly. "Can you be more specific?"

"It really is hard to explain."

"Is it about a boy? Or maybe a girl?"

"Oh no," said Undine dismissively. "I wish it were something that simple. No, it's more"—she looked at Lizard, lying on his back in the sun—"a kind of sixth sense, I suppose."

Mim raised her eyebrows but Undine couldn't tell what she was thinking. "Go on."

"Well, last time anything like this happened was when Stephen . . ."

Mim winced slightly.

"I'm sorry." The sound of Stephen's name spoken aloud was still shocking. The shape of his name hung between them for a moment, until Mim blew out a lungful of smoke with the force of a combustion engine, and it dissolved.

"So you think someone else is going to . . . get hurt?"

"I don't know." Undine studied her coffee again. "No. It's different this time. Something's going to happen. Something's going to change. And I don't want it to." Undine had surprised herself. It wasn't till she started thinking aloud, to explain the mysterious sensation in her most secret self, that the feeling began to reveal its true nature. It was the moment between dropping something—like a favorite china cup—and it hitting the ground. It was that sudden awareness of inevitability: the moment before loss, when you know something you love is going to break, or be irretrievably altered.

Mim tilted her head. "Change isn't always bad, you know."

Undine nodded, but she had to admit to herself that change, for her, was bad. She liked things to stay in their predictable patterns. She wanted Trout to stay her best friend forever, not to fall in love with her. She wanted Jasper to stay small forever, for the three of them to live in the funny little house in No-Man's-Land and visit Stephen's parents and Mim on the weekends. Most of all she wanted Stephen back, for it to be how it was when he was alive, only with Jasper as well, living as an ordinary family, with ordinary feelings in ordinary places.

"It's hard work," Mim said, "but it can be good. Change can be the best thing for everyone. Life would be a bit boring if you always knew what was going to happen."

Undine finished her coffee and Mim lit another cigarette.

"You poor thing," she said to Undine. "I can't bear

what my five ordinary senses tell me sometimes. It would be awful having another one."

"So you believe me?"

Mim shrugged. "Sure," she said, flicking cigarette ash over the side of the veranda. "Why not? Stranger things have happened."

CHAPTER THREE

Mim let Undine stay for the rest of the day. She made a comment about school, but Undine shook her head. Mim didn't push the issue. She produced a pair of baggy tracksuit pants and a long-sleeved T-shirt, and Undine gratefully wriggled out of her school uniform. She was glad to put on loose clothes and get out into the garden to do some *body* work. She weeded and planted and buried her thoughts in the garden. The feeling had subsided almost completely, and she was ready to call it a false alarm, when she heard a whisper that seemed to come from inside her, or rather, transmit through her, like radio waves through a transceiver. The sound was located just inside her ear, as if it were traveling outward instead of in.

Undine, the whisperer said. *Undine. It's time to come home.*

She glanced up at Mim, who was at the other end of the garden.

Undine . . . it's time to come home . . .

"Great. Now I've got feelings that *speak* to me." Undine viciously pulled up onion weed, taking deep breaths to slow her panicky heart. She tried singing loudly to herself. She couldn't think of one song from beginning to end, so she threaded together first lines and bits of chorus from a variety of songs to drown out the whispering voice.

Maybe I really am going mad, she thought, but though she had managed to silence the voice, or at the very least it had silenced itself, she couldn't help but consider the message. Glancing at her watch she could see it was almost three, and decided it was worth risking a slightly early homecoming. Lou was only half aware what time it was on a good day. She would have noticed if Undine had turned up mid-morning in school uniform, but it was unlikely she'd know the difference if Undine was twenty minutes early in the afternoon.

Mim's house was quiet and still. Undine went into the cool blue-tiled kitchen and helped herself to a glass of orange juice. She drank quickly. She was about to refill the glass when the whisper returned, garbling the same phrase over and over, the words rolling faster until they separated and began forming new patterns: *Undine, Undine, it's time to come home . . . time to come Undine . . . time to come home . . . Undine it's home time, time to come home . . . it's time Undine it's home time Undine come home time Undine . . . it's time to Undine . . . Undine* COME HOME!

The last two words were a shout. Her ears rang with it. She lowered her head to the bench, feeling

29

the cool marble soothe her forehead. She was still like that when the screen door snapped shut.

"Undine!" Mim's voice was panicky. "Are you all right? Undine?" (*Undine, Undine, it's time to come . . .*)

"Stop it!" cried Undine, putting her hands to her ears. "Stop it, stop it!"

Mim grabbed her arm. As soon as Undine felt her hand—the profoundly normal touch of human skin on human skin—the voice went away. "God, you're really going to think I'm crazy now," she said, almost managing a smile to reassure Mim that she wasn't. "I'm hearing voices in my head."

Mim was looking at her hand, horrified. "Oh," said Undine, her face growing pale. "I must have broken a glass." Blood pooled from a cut on her hand onto the benchtop. Pieces of glass lay scattered on the bench and floor.

"Here," said Mim. "Let's clean this up." Undine leaned over, picked up a long piece of glass, and cradled it in her hand. "No, stupid," Mim said. "Leave that. I meant let's clean you up."

Undine perched on the edge of the bath while Mim mopped up the blood and bandaged the wound.

"I look like a casualty of war," said Undine, lightly, trying to break the tight, thin wire of tension between them.

Mim forced a smile. She fastened the bandage, pulling to make sure it was tight enough. Already they could see blood petalling through the gauze.

"You don't think . . ." Undine hesitated. She was trying to translate Mim's grim silence before she spoke. "You don't think I did this on purpose, do you? You don't think I'm really crazy?" For a moment Undine wasn't even sure herself.

Mim's voice was strained as she answered. "First of all, I don't think you're crazy. Second, lots of non-crazy people cut themselves on purpose just to see what it feels like. God, even I've done that. Last of all, I know this was an accident. I just don't like the sight of blood, that's all." She smiled wanly and Undine almost believed her.

"Mim, do me a favor; don't tell Lou."

"I think she's going to notice," said Mim, adjusting the bandage.

"Come on, Mim. Not about my hand. I can explain that. About the other stuff. It's just . . . well, it's too weird for her. She'll worry."

Mim looked uncertain, her face still strained. "What makes you think it's not too weird for me?"

"You still believe me, don't you?"

"Oh, I believe you. But look what's happened to you. I can't make a promise like that."

"Please, Mim, please," Undine begged. "Don't tell Lou. I promise, if I can't handle it, I'll tell her myself. But this was just an accident. And the voice has stopped now. I might even have imagined it."

Neither of them believed this. Reluctantly, Mim agreed not to tell Lou. "But, mate, if you're getting hurt . . . just promise you'll keep me in the loop. If anything else happens, anything at all, I want to know about it."

"Are you sure it's not too weird for you?"

"Oh, it's bloody weird all right. But Undine . . .

even though, in the grand scheme of things, I'm not that much older than you, the plain fact is: you're the kid and I'm the grown-up, even if I don't always feel like one. I have to be able to deal with this. I might let you skip the odd school day, but I can't let you get yourself into any real trouble. Now, come on, I'll give you a lift home. But before we go, promise me."

Undine promised.

As soon as Lou saw Undine's hand she went into full-blown mother mode. She redressed the wound, and fluffed and flounced Undine into bed straight after dinner.

Lou loved looking after Undine when she was sick or injured. It didn't happen very often, but a delighted gleam came into Lou's eye whenever Undine had a sniffle or a temperature. Once Undine had said accusingly, "You're *glad* I'm sick! What kind of a mother are you?"

Lou had looked sheepish. "It's not that I'm glad you're sick, exactly. . . ."

At first Lou had just loved the company. When Undine was younger, before Lou met Stephen, they lived in a poky flat on the other side of the river. The flat was actually two damp, dark rooms under a house. The house was occupied by the owners of the flat, a dry, bitter old couple whom Undine remembered only as Mr. and Mrs. Pickle, though those weren't their real names. They were just bumpy and vinegary, like pickles.

Lou hated it there. The flat was always cold, even in summer, and seemed to be shrinking further and further into the ground. The Pickles' garden was overgrown, with lantana and nasturtiums strangling every spare inch. Lou had been at war with that garden. Defend, retreat, defend, retreat.

The Pickles discouraged visitors (by standing at their windows glowering at anyone who approached the house, until all Lou's friends were scared to visit). Lou *was* glad when Undine was sick, because it was lonely at home all day in the dank rooms, listening to the Pickles shuffling around upstairs. She loved having Undine in the other room while she was working. She could take a break and sit by Undine's bed, listening to her breathe, or taking her temperature. At lunchtime there would be sandwiches and soup, and Lou, who on her own never bothered with lunch, felt mothered as much as Undine.

So for Lou sickness signified secret, stolen time with her daughter. Their years in the flat had established a pattern between them, a pattern Lou cherished. Undine, who preferred not to be sick at all, was less enthusiastic about it.

But tonight Undine enjoyed the attention. She lay in bed, the feeling gnawing at her like an old enemy. She was drained, exhausted, both from the physical wound on her hand and the terrifying pressure of the otherness that had been residing inside her. That was how she thought of it now: something outside her, something *extra* to herself, that had somehow found passage into her mind, and was trickling through the cracks and crevices of her consciousness.

She dreamed of her wound. She dreamed she was peeling away layers and layers of bandage to the raw, damaged skin. The wound was clean and dry; there was no blood, but it was deeper than she remembered. She pushed the wound open, and inside there were sand and tiny shells, and miniature crabs scuttling sideways. And then, from the aperture of the injury, the whispering began, "*Undine, Undine, it's time to come home . . .*"

Lou shook her awake. Undine sat up in bed, still choking out sound.

"Undine? It's okay. I'm here. You're awake. You're home."

Undine shook her head, groggy, only partially present.

"Jesus, Undine. What were you dreaming about? You scared the hell out of me."

"Mum?" Undine was still trying to straighten out her thoughts, to separate dreaming from reality. "Lou?"

"I'm here. You must be spooked. You haven't called me Mum since you were Jasper's age."

"What are you doing up here?"

"You were shouting in your sleep. You kept yelling, 'I *am* home, I *am* home.' Must have been a ripper of a dream, sweetie."

"Mmm." Undine remembered the sensation of opening the wound and could feel the sand and the shells and the crabs moving—*living*—under her skin. She clutched the bandaged wound, shuddering.

From downstairs they heard Jasper crying. "Oops. Sounds like he's working his way past ambulance to fire engine. Come downstairs with me. We'll all get up and have a midnight feast, hey?"

Undine gathered Jasper up out of the crib. He was too big for it really, and the bars were pointless as he was perfectly capable of climbing out on his own. Lou had never got around to buying him a proper bed. Undine suspected that it was because Lou didn't want to encourage Jasper to keep growing.

Undine loved the smell of Jasper when he had

just woken up: brown-sugary sweet. His hair was damp where he had been lying on it. His eyes were sleepy and adorable. He had stopped crying, and his fingers had crept into his mouth.

"Jasper had a woogie," Jasper said, his voice still teary, muffled by fingers.

"Poor Jasper." Undine kissed the top of his head. "Undine had a woogie too." *Woogie* was a remnant of Jasper's baby-speak, when he had his own personal language for everything. Somehow *woogie* had remained in his small but rapidly expanding lexicon. *Woogie* was a safer word than nightmare; there was something comforting about it, partly because it belonged only to Undine, Jasper, and Lou. Undine held it in her mind now, like a talisman against the dark.

After a hot chocolate with Lou in the kitchen, surrounded by the dependable mess of *A Brief History of Sea Voyages*, Lou's latest indexing job, and listening to Lou read Jasper the first chapter of *Winnie-the-Pooh*, Undine felt tired enough to risk going back to bed.

This time the dream, though still disturbing, was at least more restful. She was at the beach, waves tumbling onto the shore. On the horizon, a large wooden boat keeled to and fro. Gulls arced around her, with the same harsh shriek as Jasper's fire-engine cry. She looked down and at her feet, lying on the sand, were three long bronze fish, dappled in the strange light. Someone was there, or almost there, like a ghost, printed on the air, flickering like an old film.

He thumped her hard on the chest. She woke up, gasping for breath.

When she woke, she felt ordinary again. The feeling had gone, and she thought perhaps, after all that, she had imagined it. Still sleepy, she idled down the stairs. She made herself a cup of tea, finding a meditative pause in the act of measuring out the leaves into the pot and stirring sugar into the cup. She heard the thump of the paper being flung down the steps outside from Camelot Road, and opened the front door to retrieve it. The paper was lying a meter away, but that wasn't what caught her eye.

There, on the wooden step immediately outside her own house, were three long bronze fish, dead but still fresh, their scales glittering in the early morning light.

CHAPTER FOUR

Undine burst into the Montmorencys' house without knocking. Mrs. M raised her eyebrows as Undine, dressed only in her nightie, whirlwinded up the stairs to Trout's room, nearly knocking over a half-asleep Mr. M on the way.

She flew into Trout's room and threw the one fish she had snatched up on her way out her front door onto the bed next to him. The tail of the fish slapped Trout on the face, and if he hadn't been awake before, he certainly was now.

"Is this your idea of a joke?" she demanded, her eyes glittering and furious.

"No," said Trout. "It's my idea of a fish."

"Very cute," Undine said. "And how did it get to my front door? Grew legs and walked from the sea, I suppose, with its little fish friends? I don't think so."

"Well, it does seem unlikely," Trout agreed, "but it certainly had nothing to do with me."

Undine towered over him for a moment, and he had the sudden impression of her as enormously tall, her power almost palpable in the room, like electric sparks. At the same time the thought flashed briefly through his head that Undine was in his bedroom wearing only her nightie. But the expression on her face made it clear that there was no time for a thought like that, and he pushed it aside, promising himself he would reflect on it later.

After examining his face for a moment, Undine seemed to deflate. His look of bewilderment and passivity was too much for Undine, and she was forced to admit to herself that he was not the culprit. As soon as she accepted this she realized she had never truly believed he'd had anything to do with it. After all, even if he had crept up to her house to deliver the unwanted fish, then returned to bed, how could Trout have arranged her dreams?

"Well, if you didn't do it," and her voice was small, "who did?"

Trout looked at Undine, growing and shrinking in his room like Alice in Wonderland in her vaguely transparent white cotton nightdress, and then at the fish, whose blank stare revealed nothing.

"Do you think you could start at the beginning? I'm afraid the fish is a less-than-substantial visual clue as to what the hell has been going on over the last twenty-four hours."

Undine smiled weakly. "Tell me about it."

"No," said Trout, firmly. "You tell *me* about it. What's going on? You ran off from school yesterday. You wouldn't come to the phone last night. You're behaving—excuse me for saying so—very strangely, and you've topped it all off by throwing a fish at my head. Isn't it about time you let me in on it, whatever *it* is?"

Undine sat down on the little wooden chair by Trout's bed, a relic of Trout's childhood when he used to suffer from asthma attacks and his mother would spend the night sitting by his side, managing his breathing.

"I don't know what's going on. If I did, I hardly would have thrown the fish at you, would I?"

"Well, tell me what you do know. Come on, Undine, we're best friends, aren't we?" He raised himself up on one arm, feeling rather disempowered at being in bed with the bedspread up to his neck, wearing only his jocks underneath it, while she sat at least mostly dressed looking down on him.

Undine sighed a leaky, revelatory sigh, and seemed about to launch into something, when the sound of three sharp knocks on the bedroom door startled them both. Mrs. M's voice boomed through the closed door.

"Come on, you two. It's nearly time for school. Are you *dressed* yet, Trout?"

The emphasis on the word *dressed* made them both blush.

"I better go home and get ready. I'll meet you back here in fifteen minutes."

"Well, remember to put on more than a nightie this time. You'll have my mother in an early grave."

Undine looked down at herself distractedly. "Oops."

"Oops, indeed. Now go away. I want to get out of bed and I clearly have finer sensibilities about my state of undress than you."

As she passed Mrs. M on the stairs, Undine smiled inadequately. Richard, Trout's oldest brother, emerged from his bedroom. He rubbed his eyes. "Wow," he remarked to no one in particular. "I should get up early more often."

Undine went scarlet and avoided Mrs. M's eyes, though she could hear her huffing and puffing. As Undine walked out the door, Dan was just walking in with a carton of milk.

Of course, the whole family has to see me like this, thought Undine, embarrassed.

Dan raised his eyebrows but said nothing. However, he forgot to duck at the Undine-sized door and whacked his head.

"Oh," said Undine, and, treacherously, she laughed, while it was Dan's turn to blush. Splaying her hand across her mouth but laughing still through her fingers, she flew up the stairs and burst into her own house, banging the front door behind her.

Lou observed her helter-skelter arrival. "Did you go out like that?" she asked, more amused than upset.

"Apparently."

Lou chuckled, and Undine did too, thankful her mother didn't ask for any more details. Lou looked at the fish in Undine's hand. "Did you find one too? There were two on the doorstep when I went to get the paper. Any idea where they came from?"

"No," said Undine. "Absolutely no idea at all."

"Here." Lou held out a page from the sports section

of the newspaper. "Wrap it up in this and put it in the rubbish. Good thing it's bin day today. Stinky fish is a bit much to bear, and it's going to be hot today, so *they* say."

Lou was very dismissive of *they*. *They* could be anyone, from weather forecasters to doctors, or any other disembodied group of people who had fixed ideas about things.

Undine wrapped up the fish and binned it, and went to the bathroom to prepare herself for school.

Little scales glittered on her hands from the fish, and her skin felt dry and salty. She lathered and washed, but suspected the scales were as insidious as Jasper's day-care glitter, which hung around for months, miraculously appearing underneath a fingernail or at the end of an eyelash, no matter how many baths he took, and migrating to Lou and Undine, and various other unlikely places, so that little bits of Christmas would suddenly and surprisingly appear in the corners of things. She put her hair in a messy ponytail, which actually looked all right, in a Mim way, and washed her face and hands.

It was surprising that, instead of feeling as if she might come apart altogether, Undine actually felt ready to face the day. She had a strong suspicion that whatever was happening to her was going to manifest itself as something else—like the fish—and that the feelings and the voices were gone.

At any rate, today it seemed that school and Trout were safe prospects, and Wednesdays were a slack day anyway, with double phys ed in the middle, which involved very little effort on Undine's part. Now that they were getting toward the end of the year, they were allowed to choose their own activities. Last lesson, Undine and her friends had sat on the little hill overlooking the oval, making daisy chains.

Mr. Hanson, the spunky young sports teacher, who seemed to like Undine despite her eternal lack of interest in organized exercise, had come up and said, "You know that wasn't exactly what we had in mind."

Fran had looked up with her big blue eyes and

said, "But, Mr. Hanson, we're improving our hand-eye coordination." Fran was the star of the hockey and cross-country teams, so Mr. Hanson just grunted and walked off, and they spent a happy hour clipping holes in the stalks with their fingernails, pushing the next flower through, and winding themselves in long, looping chains of the white-and-yellow flowers.

Undine had felt as if she were in primary school again: the childish activity, the almost overwhelming smell of the freshly cut lawn on the oval, and the general silliness that pervaded the group of girls, so that by the end of the lesson they were rolling around on the grass, laughing weakly, hiccupping air, unable to stop.

Undine double-checked that she was completely dressed as she left the house for school. Trout was waiting at the bottom of the steps for her.

"Come on, we'll miss the bus. You women, you take an age to get ready."

Undine gave him a playful swipe. "Oh, bollocks,"

she said. "What do you know about women? And who picks up whom every morning on the way to school?"

"Yes, yes. Details. Anyway, you should be nicer to me, Ms. Secretive. I may just have a secret of my own."

"What?"

"It's about your fish."

Undine looked at him expectantly. Trout remained silent, but smug.

"Well?" Undine asked finally. "What about it?"

"Ah-ah-ah." Trout waggled his finger. "I'll tell you mine if you tell me yours."

Undine rolled her eyes. "But if it's about my fish, then it's my secret. Isn't it? And you've . . . misappropriated it."

"Sorry. This is not negotiable. The fact is, it is my secret, because I know what it is and you don't. So spill."

"You're being childish!"

Trout smiled annoyingly. "Technically at sixteen,

in the eyes of the law, I am a child. But that's not the point. Are you going to tell me or aren't you?"

Undine made a funny noise in the back of her throat, like a growl, but Trout knew he'd won. "All right," said Undine, as the bus pulled up. "I'll tell you, but not now. After school."

"Mine can wait too," said Trout, sauntering onto the bus behind Undine. "By the way, my mum said your nightie was so transparent she could see your knickers."

Somehow Trout had timed that comment to come exactly at one of those awful, perfect moments when a sudden quiet had fallen over the bus. The word *knickers* rang through the air and the raggle-taggle of kids from the Year 7s to the Year 12s started hooting and laughing loudly, but not so loud that they couldn't hear Undine's response. They leaned forward, waiting for it.

Trout and Undine stood at the front of the bus, caught in the aisle between the smelly brown leather seats, frozen for a moment. Trout looked mortified, but Undine turned around and said serenely, "Oh well, at least I was *wearing* knickers," and the bus exploded, but somehow the laughter, which had been directed at them, turned into something friendly and easy and Trout slumped into his seat, pulsing with relief.

CHAPTER FIVE

As Undine predicted, school was comfortably ordinary.

It turned out *they* were right; it was an exceptionally hot presummer day, so phys ed was a swim in the river behind the school or, for those without bathers, a paddle. Or, for those girls who liked to live dangerously, sunbathing on the gravelly sand.

"You could go for a swim in your *knickers,*" one of the boys from the bus called to Undine as she stood ankle deep, looking longingly out at the water.

"We could, you know," said Fran, "and our T-shirts. No different to bathers."

"They'd be wet all day," said Undine, though not opposed to the idea.

"We could lie on the grass afterward and dry them out."

Not all the girls could be convinced, but Undine was easily persuaded. The idea of suspending her body in all that blue (though it looked a bit more like a mucky greenish gray up close) was too tempting to worry about leaving little damp seat marks on the splintery school chairs, and she and Fran ran in, followed by a few other squawking girls, shouting from the icy cold.

"Watch out for icebergs! The water comes straight from *Antarctica!*"

Fran and Undine bobbed about, exerting little energy, talking idly over their plans for the summer, or Fran's plans at least. Undine knew this summer would be like the last one, and the one before. Two weeks camping in the mountains with Lou and

Jasper and Mim, and various extraneous people dropping in and out, with at least one huge exhausting bushwalk to remind everyone why they live in the city and only go bushwalking once a year.

Fran was going to Noosa with her cousin and her cousin's friend. "Ah, the beach." Fran smiled up at the sky serenely. "Proper beach. Not this boring river with its barnacles and stones. The Pacific Ocean. Warm water. *Lifeguards*."

Undine closed her eyes. The sea. Lou hated the sea. She was terrified of it: sharks, riptides, the openness of it, the emptiness. She didn't mind rivers or creeks or even lakes, but, "It just stretches on *forever*," she said of the sea, with horror. "*Forever*." No one could persuade Lou to holiday on the beach and so Undine had very little experience of the sea.

But Undine was fascinated by the sea, for some of the same reasons that Lou was repelled. The emptiness. The openness. She remembered reading somewhere that sailors were called, the sea chose them.

Undine thought she might have heard this call in her dreams, the sea's siren song.

Her own name was a sea name. The book Lou had bought to choose a name for Jasper, when he was still a restless lump inside her, said *Undine* was Latin, meaning "of the waves," but Trout had told her Undine was a sea nymph in old mythology. In fact, it was one of the reasons she and Trout had become friends.

Trout had been a nickname, describing his panting asthmatic breath, but somehow it had evolved from being a private family joke to being his moniker in the outside world, so not even teachers called him by his real name, which was, forgettably, Trevor.

Trout and Undine had recognized each other from their names as two sea things, landed in the dryness of the suburbs.

Suddenly Fran gasped out a little strangled cry. "Ugh. Ooh. I think a fish just brushed past my leg."

"A fish?" said Undine doubtfully. "Are you sure?" She'd had quite enough of fish for one day.

Fran grimaced a smile. "I hope it was a fish."

"Seaweed?"

"Ugh." Fran shuddered. "Whatever it was, it gave me the heebie-jeebies. I'm getting out."

They kicked themselves back to shore and lay on the beach on their school sweaters, drying themselves out. Undine slathered herself in sunscreen and pulled her school hat over her face, sticking her legs into the shade of one of the resilient native trees that grew by the river, rooted in the sandy soil.

Conversation dried up in the heat, and Undine closed her eyes, feeling sleepy and satisfied, the salt water stretching her skin so it felt taut. She listened to the shouts bouncing over the water amidst the warble of birds, and drowsed happily.

"Hey, sleepyhead!" Fran roused Undine from her state of slumber. "Come on. It's time for lunch."

"Oh, you go ahead. I might just stay here for a while." Undine waved Fran away.

She closed her eyes again, but couldn't recapture the feeling of peacefulness she had had a moment before. She was just trying to decide if she was hungry enough to walk all the way to the canteen when she felt a shadow pass across her face.

She opened her eyes to find Trout standing over her. "Here." He pushed a bag of food toward her, doing his worst Italian mamma impersonation. "Eat somesing. You too skeeny."

"Yum," said Undine. "Your mum packs the best lunches."

"If she knew you were eating it she'd probably give me liver and arsenic."

"She doesn't hate me *that* much. Does she?"

"No, silly. She's just worried you're going to corrupt her little boy." Trout tried to make his eyes say, *Corrupt me*, but Undine was looking intently at her sandwich.

"Now," said Trout, in what he hoped was a commanding tone. "We've got fifteen minutes until class. About this secret of yours . . ." He looked at her expectantly.

Undine rolled her eyes. "Not here, Trout."

"Come on. I'm *dying* of curiosity."

"Trout!"

"All right. I was going to show you something, but it'll have to wait until after school. What class do you have now?"

"Ancient history. Exam review."

"I'm off to see Ms. Hague."

"But you're not even doing English lit this year."

"Well, aren't I mysterious then?"

"Oh, be like that. Give me a minute, and I'll walk with you."

Undine patted her almost dry knickers, and pulled her phys ed shorts on. She knew she'd get away with not being in uniform—at this time of year, the teachers were pretty relaxed about it.

She and Trout walked up to the humanities block together. Outside Ms. Hague's classroom, Trout turned to Undine. "This is where I get off," he said with a funny half wave, more a dismissal than a good-bye.

Undine smiled and turned away, but after Trout

had gone in, curiosity got the better of her and she glanced into the classroom through the interior window. Ms. Hague was wearing her *oh-how-fascinating* expression and they were both bent over, examining something quite small. Ms. Hague reached up and pulled an enormous book off the shelf. Undine knew which one it was straightaway.

"Pff, Shakespeare," she breathed aloud, dismissively. They were both mad about Shakespeare. No doubt they would be in raptures for the whole period. Undine shook her head and hurried off to ancient history, trying to make herself care who had won the Peloponnesian War.

CHAPTER SIX

On the bus on the way home, Trout kept jiggling with excitement. Undine was hot and sticky.

"Woof," she said, fanning her face. "And I think I've got problems! Those poor Greeks, having to listen to Homer waffle on."

Trout stopped jiggling and looked surprised. "I like Homer."

"You would."

"Anyway, he didn't waffle. He sang."

Undine groaned. "That's even worse. Tra la la.

And then the great hero Achilles went into an epic sulk and was boring for a very long time. Tra la la. And here's the name of every ship, all one billion of them, and everyone who was ever on each ship, tra la la."

"Your problem is you don't appreciate good poetry."

"I do appreciate *good* poetry. Just not *boring* poetry."

The bus pulled up at their stop. Undine ambled up Myrtle Street, relieved to be in the fresh air. There was something about kids en masse in small, enclosed spaces. *Way* too hot and stinky. *Eau de sneaker.* Trout jumped around as if he were about to explode.

"Come on." He pulled at her arm. "I've got something to show you."

"All right, all right. Just let's go somewhere cool. I'm cooking."

They grabbed juice boxes from Trout's fridge and went down to the bottom of his garden, which at some point stopped being his garden and started being the rivulet. It used to be skanky and ditchlike, being downstream from the old tannery, but had been cleaned up and was now quite pleasant, though Undine wouldn't like to actually come into contact with the water. Big trees swung over them, and the soil smelled damp and cool, making the air green and lush, though it was still warm.

For a moment it seemed to Undine that she was underwater, somewhere on the ocean floor, looking up at, not trees, but swathes of seaweed, drifting in the currents and eddies.

"You first," Trout said. "Tell brother Trout all about it."

"Promise you'll *listen*, though. Don't go all scientific and skeptical on me."

Undine told him everything. She began with that lumpy feeling that had come over her on Tuesday morning and ended with the fish, manifested apparently from her dreams, glittering in the weak morning sun. Trout listened carefully, and when she finished took something out of the front pocket of his bag.

At first Undine thought it was a cigar, but when Trout handed it to her, she could feel the lightness of the small cylinder and realized it was hollow.

"It opens," Trout told her.

She shook it gently, and could hear something rustle inside. A small cap came off the top and she could smell a faint whiff of tobacco. It had been made to hold a cigar, then.

There was a small scroll of paper inside. She unrolled it, took one look and exclaimed, "Trout! Is this Shakespeare? I've had enough of dead white males today. And living ones," she added with a pointed glare. She was irritable and uncomfortable in the heat, and the tops of her legs were sore where her knickers, stiff with dried salt water, had been rubbing against her. "Is this some sort of joke? And if it is, is it one I'm going to get?"

"Read it."

In small, rippling, silvery handwriting that looked like light on the surface of water was written:

Full fathom five thy father lies.
Of his bones are coral made.
Those are pearls that were his eyes.
Nothing of him that doth fade
But doth suffer a sea-change
Into something rich and strange.
Sea-nymphs hourly ring his knell.
Hark, now I hear them: ding dong bell.

"Okay, Einstein, so why am I reading Shakespeare? What's it from? What does it mean?"

"What do you think it means?"

"Trout!"

"Humor me."

"Well, I don't know . . . it's about someone's dead father, isn't it? Drowned. And he's turning into something else. Some kind of sea thing."

"So it would appear."

"But what does it have to do with me?"

"First of all it must have fallen out of the fish when you threw it on the bed. It was in my room."

"That doesn't mean—"

Trout interrupted. "*Second*, hold the paper up to the light."

Undine held the paper up against the sunlight that dappled down through the trees, diffusing around them.

"I can't see anything," she said crossly. "Really, you're starting to get on my—"

Then she saw it.

"Oh."

Trout nodded.

Inside the fibrous paper there was a watermark, like the ones on banknotes. But instead of the queen, the picture was her face, and the name *Undine* ran through the paper like a thread.

"But who . . . I mean . . . I already know my father is dead. This is hardly a revelation."

"Do you know the story of *The Tempest*?"

"No. We studied *Hamlet* in English lit."

Trout rolled his eyes. "You *can* actually just read Shakespeare, you know. It's not outlawed outside of school hours."

"Yeah, all right. Just tell me the important bits."

"Well, of course. I wouldn't want to *bore* you, much less educate you!"

"Trout! What does it have to do with my father?"

"Possibly nothing. However, this bit of the play is when Ariel—he's a spirit—is trying to trick this prince guy, Ferdinand, into *thinking* his father is dead. There was a big storm and they got separated and Ferdinand's stranded on this desert island. Anyway, at the end, Ferdinand's father isn't dead at all. They're reunited."

The world paused. Just for a moment everything stopped. Except Undine. The water on the rivulet was motionless. The trees above trembled and were still. Even the sunlight, which a second before had been shifting in and out of the leaves, appeared static. Trout seemed to flicker in and out of space. Then everything slid, in slow motion, back to the point of time she was in, and the world was normal again.

"Are you saying . . . my father's still alive?"

"It is one interpretation," Trout said. "I mean, he sort of could be, couldn't he?"

"What do you mean?"

Trout proceeded nervously. "You've never seen a grave. Or a photo, for that matter. You don't even know his name! All you have is Lou's word for it, and she's never been forthcoming with details."

"That's crazy. Lou would never lie about something like that."

Trout shrugged. "It was just an idea."

"Well, it's a stupid one. My father's dead." Undine got up, furious with Trout. "I don't want to listen anymore."

"Wait. Don't you want this?" The scroll had fallen into the grass when Undine so abruptly stood up. He held it out to her. "It's a kind of clue."

"It's not a clue. It's just Shakespeare! I don't want to hear another word about it. And don't ever talk to me about my father again!"

Undine pushed through the thick summery air, leaving Trout to recover the scroll and put the cigar case in his pocket for safekeeping.

This time if Undine had turned around, she would have seen that Trout wasn't watching her at all. And even if she had turned around, even if she'd seen his head bent to the ground, seen that one tear that threatened to spill, at that moment she wouldn't have cared.

CHAPTER SEVEN

Undine came home to an empty house. There was a note on the table from Lou: *Book group tonight. Where were you? Jasper at Mim's. Home late.*

Crap. It was her turn to babysit. Undine rang Mim's number, but there was no answer. She tried Lou's mobile but it was switched off. She'd have to grovel to everyone later.

It was still hot. The house was stuffy. She went up to her bedroom to change and, tucked up so close to the tin roof, it was like an oven. She retreated back downstairs and poured herself some apple juice, pulled the *Iliad* out of her bag and took them outside to the backyard.

The air was still and dry, though not silent. It seemed to almost sing, but Undine couldn't tell if the singing was really there, or if it was somehow emanating from her.

She flicked through her book restlessly, then lay it face down on her lap. She had to finish it before her exams but she couldn't seem to string the words together. Undine's mind was churning up thoughts so fast she was nauseous. She felt bad about forgetting it was her turn to look after Jasper. And with the immediacy of her anger gone, she felt terrible now about the way she had spoken to Trout. She knew he had only been trying to help.

The heat was becoming unbearable. It felt like an enormous weight, pinning her down. She lifted her hair from her neck and arched back to look up. There was no sign of a reprieve.

Two clouds drifted ineffectually in opposite

corners of the sky, with no apparent interest in each other, no ambition to combine their futures. All they needed, thought Undine, was to become one cloud, to draw into one thick mass, to weigh more heavily on the thin sheet of the sky. All they needed was to become something else, something other than their current selves, to bring some much needed rain.

She longed for rain. To feel it wash over her, to clean her and the dusty old world, to make everything fresh and green and sweet.

"Move," Undine breathed, willing them to travel across the sky. "Make it rain."

At first Undine didn't even notice they were moving. And when she did, it seemed impossible that she could be doing it.

She felt strange. She was dreamy, disconnected. Her brain was no longer an organ for thinking; it appeared to have another function entirely. It seemed as if she had left herself behind, her body some absurd thing on a *chair*, in a *garden* . . . senseless nouns, describing a world to which Undine didn't belong, had never belonged.

The clouds drew closer. She focused her energy on trying to knit them together, and the two clouds became one. She felt the pressure in the air rising, and the cloud grew enormous and dark. The wind chime that had been hanging limply from the beam of the veranda only moments before began to sway and resonate through the electrified air.

Without understanding what she was doing, and still distant, as though she were someone else watching from afar, Undine made it rain.

At first it was just a light froth, droplets suspended in the air, surrounding her like a fine mist. Then the rain came faster and harder. Lightning flashed in the sky, thunder rolled. A theater of war, hard bullets of rain exploding on impact. Undine was playing the weather like a savage instrument, but it seemed the instrument was becoming the player, performing its own dangerous music.

She swayed. She was losing control of the storm.

She became aware that she was standing in the middle of the garden, though she had no memory of having left her chair.

Garden, chair, her mind grabbed at everyday objects, trying to reorder her universe. She grappled with the slipperiness of her own name—*Undine, Undine*—and felt as if she might lose the meaning of it altogether. In that moment she was less girl than storm; another moment and she would be gone.

Undine, it's time to come home.

She felt someone grab her upper arms. "Undine!" Trout was shouting over the noise of the wind and rain. "Undine! Stop it! You've got to make it stop!"

As she focused on the sound of his voice, the weather subsided. The rain slowed, and again formed a fine mist around her. Gradually, the wind dropped. The chimes hung lifeless and ordinary in the dense air.

Undine looked up at Trout, who stared back, terrified.

Then everything went black and she fell.

Trout swept Undine into his arms. He carried her about two meters and then—mortifyingly—dropped her. So much for valor. He half dragged her up to her room; she was awake enough to help by doing a strange and not entirely convincing imitation of walking.

He left her on the bed and went downstairs to make her a cup of tea. It seemed a useful thing to do. The phone rang and Trout stared dumbly for a few shrill rings before answering it.

"Um . . . hello?" he said. It was Lou and she seemed peeved. She was cool and businesslike and Trout dropped the phone back on its cradle with relief at the end of the call.

Undine was awake when Trout returned to her room.

"That was Lou. The car won't start, so she's staying at her book club friend's tonight. She left a number."

"What about Jasper?" Undine asked tiredly.

"Mim's going to keep him."

Undine closed her eyes. For a moment Trout thought she'd gone to sleep when Undine opened them and asked in a small voice, "What did you tell Lou?"

"I said you weren't well and you'd gone to bed."

"With you still here?"

"I said I was looking after you."

Undine stared at the still surface of the tea. "How did you . . . ?" she began weakly, but faltered.

Trout shrugged. "I didn't, not really. I just . . . I could see the storm from my bedroom window. At first it was *localized*, I could see it over your house. Then as I was running up the stairs, it spread out over the city. When I saw you . . . it's impossible. I know it's impossible. But I could *see* the storm coming out of you. I don't know how to describe it. And besides, you were standing in the middle of it, in a deluge of rain, the wind whipping around you, and *you were dry*. The calm inside the storm. When I touched you, it was like . . . well, what I imagine a vacuum is like. Like we weren't even in space."

"I *think* it was me. But I can't describe it either. I mean, one second I just felt so hot, and I was wishing it would rain. And then somehow . . ." Undine shivered. To Trout, she seemed to be a different, smaller person, so unconnected with the Undine she had been in the garden, the Undine who made it rain, who he had seen almost overpowered by weather she had brought into existence from nowhere, from nothing.

"How are you feeling now?" asked Trout, concerned.

"Tired. Really tired. Oh!" she exclaimed, remembering. "Oh, Trout. I'm sorry I was so awful to you before. Those things I said . . ."

Trout waved his hand, flicking her apology away. "Don't mention it. I was being too pushy. But still, don't you think it's about time you had a talk with Lou? I mean, after today . . . This . . . this *power* has got to come from somewhere."

"You think . . . my father?"

Trout shrugged.

"Am I a witch? It was a pretty witchy thing to do, don't you think?"

Trout looked helpless. "I don't really know. I don't think so. I mean, it's got to be some kind of . . . *reaction*, I guess. Science has to fit into it somewhere. You can't just *bend* the laws of physics. They're not guidelines. They're *immutable*, binding *facts*."

"You'd think it would start with something smaller, wouldn't you? You know, a little cumulonimbus in the kitchen, a light breeze in the bathroom. It was a bit . . . *kaboom*, wasn't it?"

"No kidding." Trout gazed off idly, then frowned to himself a little, like he was working on an equation.

"What?"

"Well . . . it's just a theory. But maybe it did start small. Do you know about the butterfly effect? Chaos theory? You know, if a butterfly flaps its wings in China, then the weather in South America . . ."

Undine closed her eyes and nodded weakly. Trout gave up.

"Do you want me to go home? You look wiped out."

Undine's eyes flickered open. "Can you stay? Just for a while? Until I go to sleep?"

Trout nodded and within minutes Undine was asleep. He went downstairs and rang his mother, took the duvet from Lou's room and spent the rest of the night, sleeping fitfully, on Undine's bedroom floor.

CHAPTER EIGHT

Undine woke early and abruptly. The faintest smell of salt air hung in the room. She sat up, breathed deeply, and it was gone.

She could still feel the storm, every cell positively charged, coursing through her body like electricity. The hairs on her arms stood on end. It was an unsettling feeling, but not entirely unpleasant.

Trout was asleep on the floor. Undine slipped out of bed, careful not to step on him, and went downstairs. It felt strange having the house to herself in the morning, no Jasper or Lou, or the customary morning cacophony, but instead just Trout asleep upstairs. The air in the house seemed heavier than usual. She felt suspended in the silence.

She filled the fat brown teapot with hot water from the tap, swilling out leftover leaves, and propped it upside down on the sink, letting the last of the water trickle out while she fetched cups and the tea canister from the cupboard. As she put the kettle on, she thought about her father, turning the idea of him round and round in her mind, like she might examine a sparkling stone or a piece of colored glass in the light.

It occurred to her that it was strange she had never wondered about him before. She knew nothing about him, but was it because Lou had never told her or because she had never asked? Sure, there had been a time when she realized parents usually came in sets of two and she had just the one. She could even isolate it to a particular day.

She'd been about seven. She had been playing at

the park with a girl she had just met. They had been climbing together, swinging on the monkey bars. The other girl's braids had been so long they made patterns on the dusty ground when she hung upside down.

The day shone with detail. Undine could remember the pair of brown corduroy overalls she was wearing, with the word *grasshopper* sewn into the bib in bright green thread. It must have been late spring or summer because the air was warm and sweet and citrusy, and, remembering now, she could almost smell the strong, oily scent of the sunblock Lou had smeared on her face.

Undine couldn't remember the face of the other girl, just freckles, the large, spreading kind, and of course the braids. Undine had never been the type to walk up to strange kids and make instant friends, but there was something about Undine that attracted other children.

Undine could clearly remember the girl saying, in response to some forgotten thing Undine had said,

"But haven't you got a father?"

Undine shrugged in response. "No."

"That's stupid. Everyone has a mummy *and* a daddy. Even my cousins used to have one until he went away."

Undine was eager enough to please, but unable to deliver a father. "I don't." It had felt like failure.

The girl swung off the monkey bars, landing with a thump on the ground, and ran off to her mother. She came back triumphant, standing directly underneath Undine, who was still sitting on top of the bars.

"My mum says you do so have a daddy, anyway."

Again, Undine shrugged.

"Why don't you ask your mum?"

Obediently, Undine unwound herself from the metal bars, with none of the same grace as the other child, and trotted off to Lou, who gave her a piece of watermelon.

"Lou, do I have a dad?"

Lou looked momentarily stunned, before replying carefully, "He died before you were born."

Undine returned to the girl with an extra piece of watermelon in her hand. "He died," she reported, offering the melon.

Then the girl's mother had called her, and the girl had run off, dropping the watermelon on the ground. This too Undine could still see clearly, the bright pink and green of the collapsed melon against the dry, dusty gray-brown of the dirt.

And then of course, a few years after that, Stephen came along, and he fitted so naturally into the order of things that it seemed it was always meant to be that way, that she had been made to be Stephen's, that she was, in some fairy-tale way, Stephen's *true* child.

But surely, she thought now, it was strange that she had never wondered about her real father, wondered what he had been like, if he had been like her. Wasn't it strange that she had never even asked Lou what his name was? Wasn't it equally strange that Lou had never told her?

She caught sight of her image reflected in the

glass door of the microwave. She leaned in, examining her face. It had been a while since she had really looked at herself like that, noticing first the superficial, obvious features, and then the finer details: the pores in her skin, the slightly darker ring that circled her iris, the very faint crack at the corner of her eyes where she crinkled when she smiled, and where, when she became old, her skin would soften and droop, and she would wear permanent wrinkles.

Which parts of her, she wondered, came from him? Her eyes? Her hair? Lou was there in the shape of Undine's face, the same bone structure, her cheeks, her nose, her chin. Where was he? Could she locate him here, in her face? Or in the shape of her hands, her long fingers and thin wrists? She thought about the activity of cells inside her, the coded information in each one, made up of Lou and of him. Did he live there, in those cells, as information, a chain of numbers that translated themselves into parts of her? Did one of those numbers say she could make storms? Or was that a freak of nature, something she alone could do: an accident, a mistake?

"Watcha looking at?"

Undine spun around. Trout was standing disheveled at the kitchen bench, watching her study herself.

"I was just about to make some toast, do you want some?"

Trout blinked and nodded and sat down at the dining table.

"Tea or coffee?"

"Coffee. Please."

"Instant all right?"

"It's all we have at home."

Undine busied herself making breakfast, while Trout sat at the table watching. Neither of them spoke. Undine was surprised at how awkward she felt, including Trout in her early morning routine. It seemed so . . . *intimate*, especially with Lou and Jasper not home.

So when Undine heard Lou's key in the lock she

was relieved. Lou raised her eyebrows at Trout looking shy and pink with sleep, sitting at the table, eating toast. Trout shifted miserably in his chair and examined the grain of the table, as if he might somehow be transported into the strange landscape of eddying wood and knots and splinters.

"Good morning," Lou said, her voice polite, but with an edge that Trout recognized.

"Morning," Trout mumbled.

"Hiya," said Undine lightly, and Trout was sure that Undine had not detected the edge. "Do you want a cup of coffee?"

"Yes, please, Undine. Could you bring it to me in my room?"

After Lou had left the room, Trout looked at Undine, his face furrowed. "I might go."

"But I've just made you a coffee."

"Oh. Thanks." Trout took the coffee in his hands and gulped some quick scalding sips that nearly burned the roof of his mouth.

Lou was lying on top of the bed with her jeans

and T-shirt still on when Undine went in. The bed looked bare, and Undine realized that Lou's duvet was upstairs.

"Would madam like somezing eltz wiz 'er coffee?" asked Undine, in her French waiter's accent. "Some toast wiz ze vegemite per'aps, or ze snail from ze garden: lovely, fresh . . . ?"

Undine placed the coffee on the bedside table but Lou didn't smile.

As Undine turned to leave, Lou asked coldly, "'Did Trout stay the night?'"

"Yes," said Undine, immediately defensive. She didn't like what Lou was implying. "So? Is that a problem?"

"Why *wouldn't* it be a problem, Undine? You had a boy to stay over when I wasn't here. You took advantage of the fact that you had the house to yourself . . . which you wouldn't have if you'd been babysitting Jasper like you were supposed to."

"But . . . but it's *Trout*," Undine said, knowing

that that fact alone should be argument enough. "Hang on, Lou . . . what are you pissed off about, that I forgot about babysitting Jasper, or that Trout stayed over?"

Lou raised herself up on her elbow. "Do I have to choose? Because the way I see it, I've a pretty valid reason to be pissed off about both."

"But . . ." Undine was stunned. "But what on *earth* do you think I was *doing* with *Trout*?"

"You tell me. Or don't, because I'm not sure I want to know."

"That's awful! You're . . . *perverted.* I was sick, remember? Trout stayed to look after me."

"Well, you don't look sick to me."

Undine felt her mouth drop open. "God, Lou. Why are you being such a cow? I'm sorry I forgot about babysitting Jasper last night. I'm sorry Trout stayed the night when you weren't here to supervise! But—"

Lou put her hands in the air. "I don't want to hear it. As far as I'm concerned you betrayed my trust and you let your baby brother down in the process. We'll talk about this later."

"Look," said Undine, and her voice shook with anger and the threat of tears. "I don't know what your problem is, but—"

"I think it's pretty clear that my problem is *you*, don't you?"

Undine felt her head fill with a thick fog of anger, which spilled over. "Just because you were stupid enough to get yourself knocked up when you were a teenager . . . just because *you* opened your legs . . . I mean, I'm not like you. I don't have to have sex with Trout to . . . to . . ."

"You know nothing about it." Lou's face wrinkled up, confused. Incredulous. "You're making it up as you go along."

"No! Of course I don't! Of course I have to make it up. You never told me *anything*. About *him*. About my father."

Lou recoiled as if she'd been struck. She went white. "What did you say?" she hissed between her teeth.

"That's right, Lou. My father." She said the words, *my father*, with slow exaggerated enunciation. "You never said one word. How do I even know he's dead? For all I know he could be . . . could be . . ."

But she couldn't finish. Undine felt as if her lungs were buckling in her chest. She breathed in quickly. Her throat constricted and she expelled a mouthful of air in a sharp sob. Lou was looking at her with absolute and unreserved loathing.

"Just get out," Lou spat. "I really don't want to talk to you right now."

Following every impulse and instinct her body dispatched, Undine turned and ran, forgetting Trout completely. *Away*, her body said, *away*, *away*, and she ran out of Lou's room and the front door and into the world and away.

Trout watched her go. He had been obediently and mournfully sipping his coffee, trying not to listen to Lou and Undine fight. He desperately wanted to leave, but when he imagined himself sneaking out, he felt sly and mean, so he had stayed where he was and waited.

And waited. Even after Undine's sudden and unmistakable exit, he waited for her to come back. He sat as silent as he could, because he didn't want to attract the interest of Lou, who was still in her room, with her door ajar.

Trout had always felt intimidated by Lou. She was nothing like his own mother, who, though not *un*emotional, seemed to have only certain *maternal* emotions available to her. Or rather, he conceded, she was capable of containing her emotions, so that the only ones ever exhibited were the ones she permitted him to see. He could predict his mother's emotional life quite precisely. He knew what upset her, what made her happy, when she would be angry, *how* she would be angry.

Lou, on the other hand, seemed to possess an unknowable other self, some part of her not given over to mothering Undine. Trout knew it was unfair of him, to want to limit the possibilities of

Lou because she was a mother, but he did not really trust this other side of Lou. It was, in a remote sense, dangerous, because her behavior could not be predicted.

Trout lifted his cup to sip his coffee, but realized it was empty. How long ago had he finished it? How long had he been sitting here, waiting for Undine to come back?

He was in the process of standing up to leave when he heard movement from Lou's room. Before he had time to do anything, Lou appeared. He froze, and quivered like a rabbit. Ridiculously, he was halfway up and halfway down, bent at the knees over the table, a tableau of indecision.

But Lou swept past and up the stairs to Undine's room. She came back down carrying her duvet. Trout marveled that anyone could carry so large and voluminous a thing with such gravity and decorum. Lou wasn't much taller than Undine but like her daughter she was capable of conveying a sense of great height when necessary.

Right now she looked about twenty feet tall, giantlike, as if Trout could fit easily into the palm of her hand.

She didn't look at Trout, but returned straight to her bedroom. The air, which had become hurried and noisy with Lou's passage through the house, settled again, like thick sand around Trout's ears. He was still poised between sitting and standing, but he found himself compelled to sit again, unwilling to take responsibility for one course of action or another.

So it was as he was lowering himself back into the chair that Lou stuck her head round the corner. "Hi, Trout," she said, pleasantly enough. "Don't you think perhaps you should go home?"

Before he left—showing great restraint, because all he really wanted to do was sprint out the front door—he washed the breakfast things.

Outside the light was bright, and the air had a hot, lazy drone to it, like the velvety bumblebees that hovered over the lavender at the front step.

Trout blinked twice at the sun and looked around for Undine. He half expected to find her here, sitting on the steps waiting for him, but she was nowhere to be seen.

CHAPTER NINE

Undine *had stopped* running when she reached the Montmorencys' front door.

Usually when she fought with Lou, it was Trout's bedroom she ran to, but that only worked if Trout was actually in it. She balanced on the balls of her feet, considering her options. She *should* go home and rescue Trout, but she couldn't see how she could do it without making up with Lou and she wasn't ready for that.

Fighting with Lou was not unheard of, but it

belonged to another time: after Stephen had died, when they had almost grown used to him not being there, when they were learning to accommodate the absence of him, no longer fresh and shocking but a constant dull injury.

One day Lou and Undine stopped being kind to each other, stopped *babying* each other, and picked a fight instead. It was a strange, sudden, and temporary transformation. Later Lou had described it as a way of punctuating the grief, like a comma or a semicolon, a necessary transition from one stage to the next. Whatever the reason, they'd had some real doozies.

Both Undine and Lou had taken turns running away. Undine had not been very good at it, always going to the same place—Trout's bedroom—and never staying more than a few hours before Mrs. M sent her home. Lou, on the other hand, had demonstrated something of a talent for it, vanishing apparently off the face of the earth, and staying away long enough for Undine to be genuinely unsettled but not actually frightened. By the time she came home, Undine was so openly pleased to have her back that no apologies were necessary.

Those fights had been empty of any genuine malice but instead filled with raw, exposed, *identifiable* feelings. The fights themselves had meant nothing. They had both needed to yell and scream, to hate each other for a while. They needed the large gestures and extravagant emotions so they could stop feeling so *slight* and brittle and fragile all the time. They had needed to stop grieving, but they didn't know how.

But *this* fight was different. There had been something so systematic about it, so *planned*. But not like Lou had planned it. It was as if the argument had been inevitable, out of Lou's hands. That the argument had been waiting to happen, independent of Undine and Lou, and there had been nothing they could do to stop it. Instead they were forced to perform it. Undine was pretty sure Lou didn't mind that Trout had stayed the night. Trout was more of an excuse. And while she had expected Lou to be annoyed that she had forgotten Jasper, she hadn't expected . . . well, whatever *that* was.

Her foot hovered around the bottom step, but she felt suddenly angry at the thought of going home. What was in there? Lou, ready to yell some more? Trout, wanting to examine her, to dissect her like some specimen?

"So no," she said to herself, and she tried to insert some attitude. "I'm not going back. I'm going . . ." But where would she go? Who was she trying to kid? She'd go home. She always went home.

Suddenly, the Montmorencys' door opened. Richard appeared before her.

"Oops," he said, avoiding squashing Undine by lurching elegantly to one side. "What are you doing here? Trout's at your house, isn't he?"

Undine didn't know Trout's brothers very well. They had always seemed so much older than her and Trout.

"Um. Yeah. He is at my house. I kind of . . .

abandoned him. I had a fight with my mother."

Undine immediately felt very young and awkward, as if fighting with her mother was something she should have grown out of.

Richard still managed to be sympathetic. "Mothers!" he said expressively, and then glanced back over his shoulder into the house that held his own mother, as if scared she might appear. It was an unselfconscious gesture that made him seem for a moment sweet and vulnerable, so that Undine relaxed a little.

He studied her face. "I've got to go to uni; I've got an early class," he said. "Why don't you walk with me some of the way?"

"Oh, but Trout . . ."

Undine had a sudden, horrifying thought that she might not be properly dressed, she'd rushed out of the house so fast. She glanced surreptitiously down. To her relief she was still wearing the same clothes from the night before, and she'd even managed at some point in the morning to pull on her sandals, so she was perfectly respectable. She felt almost giddy with relief.

"I'm sure Trout will be fine," Richard was saying. "If I know him he'll be washing the breakfast things. Look, you don't have to come. But walking's a good antidote to fighting. It's very logical and makes lots of sense if you don't think too hard about how strange it is that we don't just fall over. Sometimes I think walking disproves the theory of gravity—because one's head is heavier than one's feet, you know—but then I never finish thinking about it enough to decide whether or not that makes sense." He frowned. "Sorry, I'm not doing a very good PR job for walking. I'm making it out to be a whole lot more complicated than it actually is."

Undine smiled shyly. "I think I can manage to stay upright and mobile at the same time."

"Good, good." Richard appeared genuinely pleased at the prospect of her company. And as they set off making benign small talk, Undine forgot about Trout and Lou, and storms and voices, and fish and feelings, and instead just concentrated on staying upright and mobile at the same time.

Undine ended up walking all the way to the door of Richard's lecture room with him. By the time they got there, she knew that the room was filled with history students, which was what he was planning to major in, and also that Richard thought Neapolitan ice cream was vaguely sinister, that he knew how to milk a goat and make porridge (but not at the same time), that he could play *Für Elise* on the piano but he didn't know his left from his right, that he couldn't ice-skate or drive a car, but he could say the alphabet backward without a single mistake, and that he was going on his first archaeological dig this summer, excavating a convict site at Port Arthur.

"I'm heading down there tomorrow afternoon. It's not very exciting, like Romans or Vikings, but it's good experience. Hopefully it will help me get a scholarship to go somewhere a bit farther away next year."

"Where do you want to go?" asked Undine, trying

to think where people went to do digs. "Egypt? Greece?"

"Scotland, actually. The islands. I rather fancy being a bit windswept and interesting . . . you know, the remoteness . . . just me and a hundred other undergraduates and the elements . . . Oh, and beer. I'm pretty sure there'll be beer."

In turn Undine shared her disappointment at never having had a guinea pig. When she was little, still at the Bellerive flat, she had hassled Lou for one endlessly. Lou finally fobbed her off with, "We'll see. Maybe in the spring."

"For years I asked her if it was spring yet," Undine said. She shook her head sadly. "But spring never came."

Richard clutched his heart. "Oh, how awful. No wonder you argued with your mother. What a cruel and pitiless woman. And yet one cannot help but admire the ingenuity of her evil plan."

Undine smiled, but weakly. She had forgotten Lou somehow. Richard had proved an extraordinarily successful distraction. It was nice. She felt at this very moment like any teenager; nothing marked her out as unusual. She could disappear, lose herself amongst the university crowd and no one would know that she was meant to be anywhere else.

A bright-faced, gray-haired woman who was even shorter than Undine pushed past them through the open door and made her way to the podium at the front of the lecture hall. Chatter subsided as she fiddled with an overhead projector.

"That's Professor Rose. I better go in." Richard held out his hand and it took Undine a moment to realize that she was expected to shake it. As her fingers touched his, she was suddenly reminded of the power of the storm; the energy of it seemed to be rushing to the place where their hands touched. She looked at him sharply. Had he felt it? She couldn't tell. She saw something new in his face. The same amused expression teased at the corners of his eyes, but it was as if he were seeing her for the first time. For a moment he seemed struck silent, then the moment passed and he was back to his own comical self.

"It has been a pleasure walking with you. Now remember, onward and upward. Or in your case, upright and mobile." He gave a flourish that was half wave, half bow, and Undine watched him go into the lecture hall. Just when she was about to turn away, he turned back, and for a moment their eyes met. Richard winked, then Professor Rose began to speak, and Richard hurried toward the bank of seats, so that from where Undine stood, he could no longer be seen.

It was only when she was halfway home that Undine realized she had well and truly missed the school bus. Trout would be at school by now, first period would have begun, and she would already have been marked absent. She began to feel sick again. Two days in a week. The school would ring. Lou would not be pleased.

She shook her head. "Upright and mobile," she reminded herself, and kept walking.

CHAPTER TEN

Undine knew, even before she opened the front door, that Lou wasn't home. The house seemed poised, giving the impression of a stalking cat, alert on its haunches.

As she opened the door the phone rang. It didn't occur to Undine to leave it, though as she picked it up she realized she was totally unprepared if it was the school. She should have let it ring. Lou was good at that, letting the phone ring off, but Undine was a Pavlov's dog, responding slavishly to the sound of the bell.

Anyway, it was only Mim. "Hi, Undine. Lou's just left here with Jasper. I was ringing to warn you that she knows you skipped school on Tuesday and she knows you didn't go today either."

"Yeah, I figured the school would have rung this morning. What did you tell her?"

"That you were a bit upset about something that happened at school so I let you hang out here with me. I don't think she believed me, though."

Undine felt guilty that Mim had lied for her. "Thanks, Mim."

"Is everything okay? Why didn't you go to school again today? Has something happened?"

Undine remembered her promise to Mim, and hesitated. "Well . . ." But what could she say? She didn't want to say anything. She didn't want to talk about the storm; she didn't want to even think about it. She wanted to forget everything. Hearing the lie in her own voice, she answered. "No. Nothing's happened."

Mim did not sound at all convinced, and Undine

thought she even sounded a little annoyed. "Lou knows something's going on. Why don't you just talk to her? She's worried about you, mate."

"Yeah," said Undine, unconvinced. "Worried." Angry, maybe. Ballistic. Not worried.

"I think you're underestimating Lou," Mim said.

She should have known Mim would side with Lou. "I think you are, Mim. You didn't hear her today. The things she said."

"Then tell me. You promised me, Undine, remember? You said you'd keep me in the loop."

"Look, there's nothing to tell, Mim. I was just . . . the feeling—it's gone, it was a mistake . . . I thought I heard something. I'm just . . . it's just normal teenage girl stuff, that's all. A mistake. I shouldn't have worried you."

"Oh, Undine . . ." Mim sighed before she hung up. "Don't burn your boats, okay?"

But Mim, as Mim herself had pointed out, was a grown-up, with grown-up responsibilities. She would feel she had to *do* something. Mim might have been able to wrap her head around the more intangible stuff. A feeling? Why not? A voice even. But generating a whole storm out of thin air? It was too implausible. Mim wouldn't buy it. She'd tell Lou. They'd think she was totally insane.

Don't burn your boats, Mim had said. But that's exactly what Mim was now, Undine thought, a burning boat—and for a moment she was overcome with a startling vision of an enormous wooden boat, ablaze, collapsing into the sea.

It took Undine a total of two seconds to decide that she didn't want to be in the house when Lou got home.

She went to her bedroom, changed into a fresh pair of jeans and a loose white shirt, grabbed some money from the jar under her bed, and left.

It was only about a two kilometer walk from Undine's house to the few blocks that made up the city center, and she took it slowly, looking into gardens, admiring the old cottages and Victorian town houses, some of them built on the downward slope, so that they had a third story below street level, almost subterranean. Many of them had been converted into offices and doctors' practices, with plaques on the door saying things like DR. FLETCHER, SPECIALIST IN DISEASES OF THE SKIN.

She stopped to talk to cats basking in the sun, patted dogs, smiled at babies, and hummed a little under her breath.

Actually, on the whole she was in a fantastic mood. Which, all things considered, was unexpected. As she investigated her good mood, her mind turned something up for further scrutiny. It was the image of Richard, looking back, winking at her.

Oh.

Thinking about that wink, and Richard's smile, her stomach capsized, and she felt a strange little tickle in the back of her throat.

Oh crap.

When it rains, it pours. Or in Undine's case, when it rains, the world flies apart.

• • •

Undine went into every shop in Hobart. Clothes shops, shoe shops, delicatessens, shops selling home wares, shops selling hardware, bookshops, music shops, little shops, and big department stores, but she couldn't find anything that she wanted. Her money was burning a hole in her pocket and she was desperate to buy something, but nothing seemed to suit.

What could she buy, what one object could make her world make sense? A hairbrush? A pair of red patent-leather shoes? A hat? It was ridiculous. She touched everything she saw, and it all seemed to resonate with a hollow echo, as though nothing were quite as real as it had been yesterday.

She felt as if she were detaching from the world, spiraling off to some other place. Everything seemed shabby, like a pale imitation of itself—as if she were on a movie set, but no one had told her her lines.

The city had that deserted weekday air about it. It was as though everyone except Undine was where they were supposed to be. It was kind of exciting.

Possibilities seemed to expand around her, although she didn't quite know what those possibilities were.

As the day passed into the afternoon she wandered down to Salamanca, which on Saturdays was a big marketplace, and every other day was a parking lot. Except for the cars, Salamanca felt out of time, with its cobbled ground, the huge stone buildings and, opposite them, the lawns and the large English trees, threaded with fairy lights that were lit at night. The sandstone buildings were filled with cafés, restaurants, and galleries, and arcades of permanent shops were sandwiched between them, selling art, crafts, antiques, furniture, and second-hand clothes and books.

It was all so artificial. It was beautiful, but it did not belong to her. She was a tourist, an outsider, and she could only see the thin surface veneer of things; she couldn't get beneath it to the real heart of anything.

She called on all her senses, trying to find a way in: looking at mirrors and masks and hand-blown glass bottles and soaps carved to look like shells; fingering bright, lumpy candles; stroking the thick coarse wool of handmade sweaters and the soft mohair of knitted hats; brushing hand-dyed silks against her cheek. She cradled heavy-based pottery jugs with fine cracked-egg glazing, and opened and closed wooden boxes: myrtle, blackwood, Huon pine, breathing in their sharp, sweet perfumes.

She lingered outside the cafés and bakeries, inhaling the aroma of freshly ground, roasted coffee and the yeasty smell of baking bread. She admired jars of small cheeses marinated in oil, and chilies, olives, and dried tomatoes, displayed in the long wooden-framed windows of a restaurant.

She bought a souvlaki and sat on the grass to dismantle it, extracting the hot spicy meat blackened on the spit, licking the garlicky yogurt off her fingers, pulling apart the bread to eat with slices of tomato but discarding the ubiquitous shredded lettuce. Seagulls collected around her, and she tossed them the unwanted lettuce and the soggy remains of the bread.

The sun glistened and shone, and the day

stretched around her like a bubble, protecting her from what had happened and from what might happen, holding her in the here and now. She felt a taut sensation in her tummy, as if she were waiting, balanced on a precipice, about to dive in and discover a new world. It was dizzying.

She lay down on the grass and closed her eyes, feeling the late afternoon sun on her face. She listened to the birds, to the sound of car doors closing and engines revving, and to the music, chatting people, and clinking glass at the pub across the road where the after-work crowd were spilling over onto the footpath. She could hear the faint *swish* of the leaves above her. A child shouted. A car horn blazed. A ship sounded in the nearby river docks. She could hear it all so clearly, and yet it was all so far away. She had the uneasy sensation that she did not belong to this world anymore, that the magic she had done had separated her from the rest of the living, breathing populace of the city.

And then, softly, "Undine . . ."

. . . Undine, it's time to come . . .

"Not you again," Undine said crossly and sat up.

Richard was standing over her. "Sorry." He looked red in the face.

"Oh no, not you, I thought you were . . ."

Who, Undine? she asked herself. The voice inside your head?

It was strange that she hadn't realized until now that the internal voice had been there all day, like the humming of a fridge in a kitchen, a background noise to which she had learned to pay no attention.

". . . someone else."

Richard smiled. "You looked like you were sleeping."

"Just about."

"Sorry to wake you."

"Oh no, no, that's okay."

They shared a moment's awkward silence. Undine had to squint to look up at Richard, who was standing just to one side of the lowering sun.

"Shall I sit down?" Richard asked. "Your face is all scrunched up. It looks painful."

"It is a bit. If you take two steps to the left I should be all right."

"Like this?"

"Lovely."

"Having gone to all that trouble," Richard said, "I actually have to go. I'm meeting people in the pub. Do you want to come?"

Undine hesitated. "Um . . . I'm underage."

"Oh yes," said Richard, breezily, "so you are. I'm sure we can smuggle you in. There'll be a group of us. Duncan's girlfriend is underage too."

"Yes, Fran. I know her."

"Well, there you go. Coming?"

Undine had had alcohol before. Lou gave her a glass of wine with dinner sometimes, and she'd had the odd beer at parties, but she'd never been to the pub before, mostly because she was worried about getting caught.

She looked at Richard's face, the setting sun framing it. She should go home. She should make up with Lou.

But suddenly she was overcome by the desire to try to slot herself back into the human race, to prove to herself that she was no different from anyone else. To be an ordinary, irresponsible teenager, like Fran.

Richard offered his hand and pulled her to a standing position.

"Coming?" he asked again.

Undine smiled. "Sure."

Chapter Eleven

It *turned out that Richard's* friends were the sort to start early, so they actually had a table inside. As they pushed their way through the burgeoning crowds, Undine kept her face down.

After spending the day alone, it was strange to suddenly be in the middle of a lively throng. Despite the friendly atmosphere of the crowd, Undine still felt remote and disengaged, as though she was an observer only, and not a participant. It didn't help that she was underage—she was sure it was written all over her face, and she avoided eye contact with the smiling beery men they passed, in case one of them was an undercover policeman, about to leap out and arrest her.

"Hi, everyone," Richard said, stopping at the biggest table. "This is Undine." Richard ran through about a dozen names, gesticulating around the table. Undine recognized a few people, including Duncan and Fran, whose face lit up when she saw Undine, and Dan, Trout's other brother, who shot Richard a questioning glance.

Fran shuffled over on the bench seat she was sharing with Duncan, elbowing him as she did so.

"Here, Undine, sit next to me."

"Do you want a drink?" Richard asked her. It was noisy in the pub and he had to lean over and talk right into her ear. His voice reverberated through her ribcage. She felt him brush against her hair and her stomach quivered and seemed to rise and drop like a jellyfish. She could smell his skin, not unlike the smell of Trout's—Oh, Trout, she thought with a pang—but Richard was sharper, *sexier*. She looked down at the table, hoping no one had noticed the effect he had on her.

"Yes, please."

"Beer?"

Undine nodded.

Fran said, "Where's Trout?"

"Um. He's not here." Poor Trout. She felt hideously guilty, not just for walking out on him, but because she hadn't thought about him all day. Thinking about Trout might lead to thinking about the storm, and about her fight with Lou, and that was no good. She shook her head, and tried to immerse herself in the light banter that batted around her at the table.

Fran was studying her too closely. "I thought you and Trout were, you know . . ."

"Did you really?" Undine was genuinely surprised. She considered Fran to be one of her closest friends, but it occurred to her that they never really spent much time together out of school.

"I mean, I know you deny it at school . . ."

"No, no. Trout and I are just friends, really."

Duncan leaned over Fran and smiled. "Isn't that what they all say?"

"Oh *they*," said Richard, who was suddenly standing at Undine's shoulder. "What do *they* know?"

"Oh my god," Undine groaned. "You should *so* meet my mother."

The guy sitting across from Undine, whose name was Grant or Grunt or something, made a sound like a whip. "Watch out, man," he said to Richard. "She wants you to meet her mother."

"Oh yes," said Richard. "Very droll." But Undine could see he was uncomfortable. He handed her a beer, and went and sat down at the other end of the table with Dan and a rather pretty blond girl, who flicked her hair at him.

"Don't worry about Grunt," Duncan said, leaning over Fran. "They still haven't figured out how to connect all three brain cells."

"What?" said Grunt, stupidly. Fran and Undine laughed.

"So anyway, Miss Naughty," Fran nudged her. "Where were you today?"

"Oh," said Undine, with a grin. "Whoops."

"What's this?" Duncan asked.

Fran raised her eyebrows at him. "She wags school, then she shows up at the pub."

"What a rebel!" said Duncan. "I don't know if I want you hanging around with her, Fran. She might be a bad influence."

"Yes, Mum! Anyway, Undine could wag the whole year and still get great marks."

Exams! Undine groaned inwardly, and then with an enormous mental effort, heaved studying into the same closed box already occupied by Trout, Lou, possibly Mim, and the storm of the previous night. "I wish," she said, lightly. "I think my math teacher might have something to say about that. If he could get the words out while he's choking with disbelief."

"Ah, math teachers," Duncan reminisced, "the great unbelievers."

• • •

Undine and Richard walked silently together up the hill.

It was dark by the time they left the pub, but Undine didn't care. She felt fuzzy from the two beers she had drunk, the first slowly, with small, sour sips, the second with less discomfort. Beer, she had decided, was good. Beer was her friend. Beer kept everything at arm's length. It was so much easier to trivialize her world when she had beer on her side.

She would even say she had developed something of a taste for it. Not enough to want to drink it every night, but a taste for beer was useful, as it was the cheapest of drinks, apart from some nasty fruity things that were not socially acceptable, except at exclusively female Year 8 slumber parties.

She was extremely aware of Richard beside her. The warmth of his body seemed to emanate toward her even though they were not touching.

Duncan and Fran had offered her a lift home.

"It's okay. It's a nice walk. I'll be all right."

"You are *so* not walking home on your own," Fran had insisted.

"Of course she isn't," Richard had said, appearing behind Undine. "She's walking home with me." From where she was standing Undine hadn't been able to see him, but she could *feel* him and the sound of his deep voice vibrated around her and made the hairs on the back of her neck stand on end.

Duncan and Fran had subtly dissolved at that point, after Fran had given Undine a hug and said, "I'm so glad you came tonight," into Undine's ear.

Two minutes later Undine realized why Fran had been so glad of her company. Left alone with Richard and a few others, including Dan and the hair-flicker, Undine realized how out of place she would have felt if Fran hadn't been there. They stood around talking about university and exams and Richard's upcoming archaeology trip. There were others in the group going on the trip, and Undine tried to suss out whether one of them would be the blond hair-flicker.

"What do you study?" the hair-flicker had asked Undine. Dan had answered for her.

"She's in Year 11. With Trout."

"Oh. Lucky you. Trout's such a sweetie. Unlike his big boofhead brothers."

"Watch it," said Richard, and they had started a jokey slanging match, thinking up various insults for each other. It was a game that Richard and the blond girl had obviously played before, and it was one that excluded Undine. She stood silently waiting for them to finish, feeling prudish and prim.

Dan seemed to notice but did nothing to help her, and as the game drew to a close, he pulled Richard to one side. This was even more awkward than watching Richard and the hair-flicker's game; at least that had been a public display, something she could watch, so that to the outside observer she might have appeared part of it. Dan and Richard's angry murmuring in the corner was obviously not for her to hear, and though she tried clumsily to engage the blond girl again—"What's your major?" seemed the standard opener for uni students—the girl either didn't hear her or deliberately ignored her and

Undine was left with her poor discarded question hanging in the air. It may as well have been painted in fluorescent colors, she felt so obviously out of place.

Now she was finally alone with Richard, which had felt so easy and natural only this morning, but with Richard's silence, it suddenly seemed awkward and painful. She wondered if the blond girl was Richard's girlfriend, but she didn't know how to ask. Maybe that had something to do with why Dan was so wild with Richard.

They were not far from home when Richard broke the silence. "Did you have fun tonight?"

"Yes." Undine only half lied, because it had been fun before Fran and Duncan left. Surprisingly so. Undine had achieved what she would have thought impossible—feeling like a fun, frivolous teenager.

Richard became distracted again, and Undine wanted to leave it alone, but her mouth opened before her brain kicked in. "Is everything okay?"

As soon as she asked it she wanted to take it back,

because she wasn't really sure she wanted to hear the answer.

"Dan had a go at me."

"Yes," said Undine. Dan had also given her a rather greasy look as he left, after declining Richard's invitation to walk with them in favor of a ride in Grunt's car, which was a surprisingly cute little Fiat-y thing. Undine thought it better not to mention the look.

"Are you and Trout . . . ? I mean, are you . . . ?"

"What?"

Quietly Richard said, "Dan seemed to think I was stealing you away from Trout."

Undine bristled. "No one is stealing me away from anyone. I'm not a *thing*. And I am not Trout's girlfriend. Trout and I have never been anything but friends. We haven't! Despite what Fran and my mother and Dan and . . ." She looked at Richard, her anger diminishing, replacing itself with disappointment. ". . . and you might think."

"What about Trout?" Richard asked. "What does he think?"

Undine shook her head. "I can't help what Trout thinks. But I have never said or done anything to make him think we're anything more than friends."

They reached Richard's house. They lingered outside, silence hanging between them. "Look, I can't say that I don't care what Dan says, or what Trout thinks," Richard said. "I do care."

"So do I."

Richard looked into her eyes. The buzz between them intensified. She stopped feeling like an awkward, inexperienced teenager. She looked him in the eye and held his gaze.

They seemed to be getting closer together. Neither of them appeared to be moving but now their faces were almost touching.

"Dan thinks you're trouble," Richard murmured.

Undine smiled, a wry, sideways smile. "That makes me sound so exciting."

"I think you're exciting." His voice was still soft, mesmerizing—or mesmerized.

"Your mum isn't exactly my greatest fan either."

"That's only because you've got sexy legs."

Undine laughed. "I have to go. I still have a fight with Lou to repair."

"All right," Richard whispered. She felt his nose brush her cheek. "Off you go then."

Neither of them moved. Then Richard leaned in and kissed her.

CHAPTER TWELVE

There are two ways for a star to die.

A star more than eight times the mass of the earth's sun will become a supernova. It will burn hot and blue until it exhausts the hydrogen at its core; then it will burn helium, then carbon, neon, oxygen, and finally silicon. Silicon burns into iron and iron does not burn at all. The star runs out of energy and explodes and collapses, shining with the light of a billion suns, spinning in space, pulsing like a lighthouse. A smaller star will gradually shed its outer atmospheres and form a bubble of expanding gas around itself, becoming cold and dense, what's known as a white dwarf.

Trout, whose feelings for Undine seemed to burn inside him, thought of his heart as an enormous star, pulling about it masses of energy. He had always supposed that his love for Undine would eventually burn everything he had, all his resources, and that one day his heart would supernova, leaving an absence that would be as present as a living sun, his damaged heart spinning and pulsing with light.

Instead, when he saw Richard lean in and kiss Undine, his heart sealed over. It became cold as liquid nitrogen.

He watched her say good night, and turn and bound up the stairs toward him, not seeing him where he sat like an obedient puppy outside her front door in the shadow of her house. He had been sitting there for how long? An hour. More. He wished desperately that he could make himself disappear. Whatever it was that was forming around his heart thickened and seized him when she did notice him.

"Oh, Trout," she said, and she was *sorry* for him, he could see sympathy all over her face. He couldn't bear it. He stood up and pushed past her, hating her, and stumbled down the stairs, almost falling.

The front door slipped in his hand and slammed, bringing his parents from the living room, the somber murmur of the television news seeping out with them. Richard stood frozen on the stairs, his hand on the banister, his features arranged in an almost comical imitation of the expression Trout had just seen on Undine's face.

Trout wanted to pull him from the stairs down onto the hall floor, to pummel him with his fists like he had when he was a small boy. But now, as then, Trout knew he would have no effect on Richard. Richard could not be hurt by his younger brother. Richard would always be older, bigger, stronger. And besides, his mother would pull Trout off, and then scold not Trout but Richard, because Trout was the youngest and his asthma made him weak.

Worse, Trout imagined hitting Richard with everything he had, and Richard laughing. And in his mind he could see Undine laughing as well, splitting the veneer of sympathy that she wore for him.

Richard opened his mouth to say something. Trout felt a spasm of anger. "Don't speak to me," he hissed.

"What's going on?" Mrs. M asked, looking from Trout to Richard. Richard looked at Trout.

"Leave it, love." Mr. Montmorency put his hand on his wife's shoulder. "Let them work it out."

Mrs. M waited, looking questioningly at Trout.

Trout shook his head. "Nothing's going on. I'm going to bed."

Richard followed him up the stairs. "Come on, Trout. We have to talk about this."

Trout turned around and for a moment he got what he thought he wanted. The expression on his face wounded Richard, and Trout realized for the first time that there were new ways to hurt his brother.

"I said"—Trout spoke through clenched teeth—"don't talk to me."

Trout closed his bedroom door and went to the window. Undine stood at her front door, where he had left her.

He stood there for some time watching her front door, even after she had disappeared inside the house, his hands shaking, his chest aching with loss.

Lou was already in bed when Undine came inside. Undine stood outside Lou's door, hoping Lou was waiting up for her. What Undine really wanted to do was slip into bed beside Lou, like she used to when she was little, and lie there listening to Lou breathe.

It bothered Undine that she hadn't had a chance to make up with Lou before she went to bed. It was rare for an argument to go unresolved between them for more than a few hours.

Undine put the kettle on and sat at the kitchen table. Her brain felt like a clothes dryer. The dueling images of Richard, his face so close to hers in that moment before he kissed her, and Trout, his face twisted with betrayal, fought for her attention.

Then her eyes caught the page-three headlines in the newspaper that lay open in front of her, and she forgot both of them.

FREAK STORM CATCHES
WEATHER WATCHERS BY SURPRISE

Last night's storm "appeared to come from nowhere," said baffled weather watcher Bill Wells from the Commonwealth Scientific and Industrial Research Organization (CSIRO). The Bureau of Meteorology today released satellite images tracking the storm's development. Wells says they prove the storm was impossible to predict.

"You can see from the images that the storm formed very quickly in a highly localized area on the fringe of the city. This is unusual as storms in the Greater Hobart area usually move in from the coast.

"The clouds formed quickly, which is also uncommon. The temperature rose suddenly just before the storm, which vanished as fast as it appeared."

Bill Wells believes the storm was simply an unusual weather phenomenon, caused by a sudden rise in atmospheric pressure. However, he does concede it may have been caused by environmental changes due to global warming and the greenhouse effect.

The sudden storm brought down trees, caused confusion on the roads, and blacked out power in some metropolitan areas, but so far no injuries have been reported.

Next to the article there was a photograph of Bill Wells looking suitably baffled and an incomprehensible reproduction of the satellite image, showing storm clouds like beaten egg whites frothing over the sky.

Undine read the article a few times over. She had avoided thinking about the storm all day, and it had become so unreal for her that she had almost managed to disown it. But here it was, written all over Bill Wells' face.

I should *do* something, she thought helplessly. But what? Send a bunch of flowers and a note of apology to the CSIRO? Turn herself in to the Bureau of Meteorology?

In the end she did the only thing she could do. She went to bed.

It occurred to Undine as she was lying in bed that maybe her father was a ghost.

The disembodied voice could be a haunting, and she supposed the storm could be some kind of psychic energy. She concentrated on the storm, trying to remember the moment when it began, when she realized she was conducting it.

Conduct. It was just the right word because it had two meanings. It could mean conduct like an orchestra conductor; they made things happen, they told the orchestra what to do. Or there were conductors like those used to conduct electricity: acted upon, merely enabling the passage of energy. So, she wondered, which was she?

The idea of her father being a ghost made the message she had been hearing even more disturbing. *It's time to come home.* When she had first heard it at Mim's, she had assumed it meant this house, the only home she really knew, except maybe for the flat in Bellerive. But if he was a ghost, then . . . what? Home. What was home to a ghost?

Her eyes drooped, heavy with sleep. Just before she dozed off, the image of Richard's face appeared behind her lids, as though printed in her memory, and she smiled, Trout, for a moment, forgotten.

Somewhere in the back of her mind, the voice kept whispering. *"Undine, Undine, it's time to come home . . ."*

CHAPTER THIRTEEN

Undine dreamed she was drowning.

Small bright fish poured from her mouth. Her hair twisted behind her like a trawler's net. Above she saw the surface of the ocean, sun playing on the sheet of blue. The wooden keels of boats, like reverse shark fins, sliced through the water.

She descended, sinking farther and farther below, past the gannets diving for fish, where the water was dark and cold, where old forgotten wrecked ships collapsed into the ocean floor, spilling their cargoes of silk and spice and tea.

Down there, residing in the empty hull of a ghostly ship, were drowned sailors. They were not quite dead, but instead had become another type of sea creature: bloated, spongy, their eyes growing sideways, the narrow slits of gills appearing on their swollen throats.

Undine panicked. She kicked, suddenly aware that she was unable to breathe. She tried to propel herself upward, but realized the dress she was wearing was weighted with stones that had been sewn into the lining. She desperately tried to pull open the stitches, but they wouldn't come apart, so she tried to slip the dress off over her head. She got caught in it, and struggled violently. Her chest burned. Her mouth opened and, with horror, she began to breathe in mouthfuls of bitter, salty water . . .

She had to fight herself awake.

She lay alone in the dark, flooded with terror. She could feel her heart thumping rapidly. She lay there, trying to breathe normally, struggling to make herself feel ordinary again.

In the dark the voice was almost comforting. *Undine*, it whispered. *Undine. It's time to come home.*

Undine must have slept again, because the next thing she knew, Lou was standing over her.

"Since you're not going to school again today," she was saying, "you can look after Jasper. He's got the flu or something. Day care won't take him if he's sick, and I've got things to do."

"I was planning on going to school." Undine was only just awake and slightly confused at the direction the conversation seemed to be taking.

"They told me on the phone yesterday that there were no classes today. Swot vac for your exams, isn't it?"

Exams. Oh lord.

"Yeah. I forgot."

Swot vac was a week off, six school days including that Friday, to study for exams. The school library was open and teachers were available, but attendance wasn't compulsory, so practically no one went.

Undine sat up and wiped her eyes. She felt bleary and strange, either due to her harrowing night's sleep, or the beer, or the events of the day before.

She looked at Lou's face and tried to figure out if things with Lou had righted themselves. Lou looked pale and trembly, as if she might have flu too. She didn't smile at Undine, and gave no sign that the quarrel between them was over.

"Right," Lou said briskly. "I'm off then. You'll look after Jasper?"

"Wait, Lou, I . . ."

But Lou was gone.

Undine swung herself out of bed, ready to pursue Lou down the stairs. "Ugh," she said as her foot landed on something damp. She looked down and there on the floor was a small pile of coarse yellow sand containing fragments of shell and a fine, beaded strand of seaweed. Beside it rested a thin, long-boned skeleton. It seemed to be some kind of bird, or parts of a bird: tapered sternum, arched pelvis, the slender hooked bone of a lower jaw, all washed smooth by the tide.

And like the previous morning, she detected a strong but brief smell of salt, wind, and kelp. She took a few quick breaths and the smell was gone.

Downstairs the house was quiet except for Jasper sniffling in his crib. Undine went to see him, but he began to grizzle sleepily as soon as he saw her and she thought it might be better to leave him alone for a while.

She made herself a cup of tea and some toast and sat at the kitchen table. Last night's newspaper was gone, replaced with Friday's. She flicked the pages disinterestedly, but was unable to absorb even the headlines.

Jasper woke sometime after nine, very sorry for himself. "I'm sick," he announced sadly over the bars of the crib when Undine went to scoop him out, though he was quite capable of clambering out on his own.

"You sure are."

Jasper chewed mournfully on toast and together they watched the kids' programs on morning television. Jasper's face was hot, his cheeks flushed red, and he leaned heavily against Undine. It was not unusual for Jasper to be sick—he picked up any number of bugs at day care—but today Undine found herself enjoying his presence, this slightly wilted, damper, softer, and more compliant version of Jasper.

Still a few hours later, the novelty of caring for sick Jasper began to wear thin. The television failed to hold Jasper's—or Undine's—attention, coloring books and modeling clay quickly lost their appeal, cars and dinosaurs and balls were pushed aside, and Jasper wandered restlessly, grizzly and bored of being inside.

After an early lunch of white bread soaked in chicken soup, Undine had a moment of inspiration and built Jasper a cave, suggesting they play hibernating bears. They crawled in together and Undine cuddled Jasper, still all snuggly in his flannel pajamas, until he fell asleep. She dismantled the cave around him and picked him up off the floor. She knew it defied the laws of gravity but somehow Jasper always seemed a lot heavier when he was sleeping. She transferred him easily to the crib and crept out, closing his door behind her.

And suddenly, though only minutes before she had desperately wanted him to be asleep, she found herself absurdly missing him. The house seemed empty and silent without his presence.

She mooched around the rooms, wondering at turns when she would next see Richard, the thought of which made her both sick and excited at the same time, and when she would next see Trout, which simply made her feel sick. Was there anything she could say to Trout to make it right between them?

She rehearsed such conversations in her mind, and they would start off well, until she seemed to lose control of even her pretend Trout, and in her mind he would push past her like he did last night, his face ugly with resentment and betrayal.

In the end, feeling entirely unqualified to manage her own life, and for want of anything more productive to do, she decided to study. She switched the television on as a study aide.

By the time the midday soap started, she'd forgotten all about exams. The show was about unlikely people called Blake and Thorn and Charity. They seemed caught up in a love triangle in which Charity loved the wrong brother. Undine found herself feeling quite sympathetic toward poor Charity, with her bleached hair and overplucked eyebrows.

She sank into the couch, ready to share Charity's heartbreak, when the doorbell rang. She froze for a minute, feeling caught, as if the person might have X-ray vision and could see her wallowing in the awful presence of daytime television.

It was Richard.

He came in and sat, not at the kitchen table where most guests sat, but on the arm of one of the ratty old couches that crowded the television in the corner. Undine surreptitiously killed the show as

Charity said, "Oh, Blake, can't you see it would never work for us?"

She stood beside him. With him perched on the couch, their eyes were level. There was what could only be described as an awkward silence. Without Richard's elegant and witty banter, Undine realized she was at a loss for something to say. *Am I boring?* she thought suddenly.

She was about to offer coffee—neither witty nor scintillating but it did promise ensuing busyness to fill the ragged hole of silence—when he took her by the hips, brought her toward him, and kissed her. She inhaled quickly at the unexpectedness of it, gasping the air right out of his mouth, and then felt like a complete idiot. Richard only kissed her harder.

It was not unlike the kiss of the night before, and yet there was a palpable difference. She realized that last night's kiss had been a good-bye kiss, and therefore finite. But this kiss had the potential to go forever, or at least for a few hours, in which case, she suspected, it would turn into something else. She felt a tingling anticipation at the thought of what that might be. Part of her wanted to give in to it completely. But she wasn't ready to let go of herself. After the storm, the thought of losing control made her nervous.

Undine felt in need of some air. She pulled away. Richard's eyes remained riveted on hers and she found she had to look away to regain her composure.

"So," Undine began uneasily, "how's Trout?"

Richard cleared his throat nervously. "Not so good. I think. He's not really talking to me."

"I don't think he's talking to me either."

Richard looked away and grimaced. "I should never have kissed you."

Undine didn't know what to say. Why was Richard here? To kiss her and then tell her he shouldn't kiss her? She moved away and sat at the other end of the couch.

Richard followed her with his eyes. "Are you sorry I kissed you?" He sounded almost cross. "Because it sure felt like you were kissing me back."

"Oh god, no. I mean yes. I was." Undine was finding this conversation agonizing. She covered her face with her hands, peering out at him sideways. "I mean, I'm not sorry. I'm glad you kissed me." She wanted him to kiss her again.

Richard slid over the couch toward her, smiling slowly, and pulled her fingers away from her face one by one.

"I should *never* have kissed you," he said, and leaned in.

She wasn't really aware of how they went from sitting side by side on the couch, kissing, to lying on the couch, Richard mostly on top of her. His mouth tasted sweet and fresh, like spring water, and his skin smelled spicy and warm. She relaxed into the rhythm of their kissing.

She became aware, or some small conscious part of her became aware, that Richard's hands were beginning to explore her body, moving over, and then under, her top.

"Undine," he murmured.

"Richard." She pushed him. "Richard, we should probably stop."

"Do you want to?" he asked throatily.

"No."

"Neither do I."

"But we should anyway."

"Should we?"

"Yes," said Undine firmly. "We should."

But Richard's hands kept pushing at the folds of fabric. She could hear his breath, rasping erratically in her ear. For a moment she thought he was going to force himself upon her.

"Richard!" she said forcefully. "No!"

He sprang up and groaned loudly. Undine sat up too.

"God, Undine," he said, and prowled around the couch like a caged animal. "What have you done to me? I've never felt like this before."

It should have been . . . romantic, but it wasn't. He sounded almost angry, as if he really thought she *had* done something. This wasn't how it was supposed to be. Why couldn't he kiss her the way *she* wanted him to?

Undine took his hand. He flinched, as if burned. She saw herself—not her regular self, but the girl who could harness the power of a storm—reflected in his eyes. And this time it was different.

Power surged through her hand to his. She was in control, not Richard. She was making this happen. He would do whatever she wanted him to do. She pulled him down to sit beside her. She kissed him— she kissed *him*—fiercely. He seemed to dissolve, to surrender, not just his body, but his will. Undine felt it, the same way she had felt tame air pass through her and become transformed by her body into the storm, dangerous and wild. *She* was dangerous, potent, and strong. Richard was weak. She almost, for a moment, despised him for it.

Neither of them heard Lou come home. Suddenly she was there, over them like a great wild bird, filling the room.

It was compromising. There was no doubt about that. Though both fully clothed, Undine was more on Richard than off him. Undine knew what it looked like to Lou.

"Get out," Lou said.

Richard flinched. He looked ashen. He looked half dead.

Undine still felt the power coursing through her. The presence of Lou seemed to have broken its thrall for Richard, but the magic didn't dissipate. It wanted to spill out from her and it took all her physical power to keep it in. Undine avoided looking Lou in the eye, frightened that Lou would see her transformed.

Richard didn't look at Lou either, just slunk out of the house and was gone.

"Nice guy you've got there," Lou jabbed. "At least Trout had the decency to stick around."

Anger fueled the magic inside her as effectively as throwing petrol on a fire. The effort of containing the magic was superhuman. She almost vomited, buckling over.

"Oh my god!" There was sudden, genuine concern in Lou's voice, and some small interior part of

Undine wanted to bend to it, to collapse into Lou. "What's wrong? Undine, are you sick?" This was her chance to let Lou in. But the magic surged and bowed in dizzying waves.

"Nothing," Undine snapped. "Nothing. Get away from me."

Lou backed off. "Fine," she said, quietly. "Undine, go to your room. I don't want to look at you right now."

As Undine limped up the stairs she felt the magic drip away, leaving only the tired knowledge that somehow her relationship with Lou had moved to a stage that was practically beyond repair.

CHAPTER FOURTEEN

"Trout?" his mother called as she heard him on the stairs.

"What?" He stood where he was on the top stair, even though he knew he was being summoned.

"Can you come in here for a minute?"

He stomped down the stairs, feeling petulant yet powerless.

"What?" he asked again, standing in the dark heavy oak doorway, looking into the kitchen.

Mrs. M had her head in the oven. She was prodding

a large garlicky beef roast, the smell of which filled the kitchen.

The kitchen was Trout's favorite room. It was built so that it came off the rest of the house, like an afterthought. There were windows sweeping around the three external walls so that light poured in. There was a long Tasmanian oak table in here where they usually ate, sitting on heavy pine benches which gave off a sweet, slightly oily smell.

"Can you set the table, please?"

It was only just past midday and the thought of having to eat that meal made Trout's stomach churn. He huffed his way over to the kitchen drawer, where the cutlery was kept.

"No," said his mother. "Not the ordinary cutlery. We're having a special good-bye meal for Richard in the dining room."

"Good riddance," Trout muttered.

Mrs. Montmorency shut the oven door. "What's that supposed to mean?"

"Doesn't matter."

"I know something is going on with you boys. Why don't you ever talk to me?" His mother's voice was plaintive.

"It's nothing. Really."

Trout felt vaguely sorry for his mother. She had once been the center of the universe to all three boys, but the universe had changed—grown colder but bigger, thought Trout, more immense with possibilities. They no longer orbited around her, but around their own things. Or around Undine, Trout thought bitterly. At least two of them did.

Sometimes, in certain lights, his mother looked old and ineffectual, as if, like the Singer sewing table that was covered in vines in the backyard, she had outgrown her usefulness. She was not attractive like Lou, but small and round and mother-hennish.

"I know something's going on." Mrs. M frowned, and her face, all slanted downward like that, looked so unappealing that Trout's sympathy instantly dissolved. "It's that girl, isn't it?"

Trout bristled, feeling defensive of Undine despite himself. "I don't really want to talk about it."

Mrs. M kept frowning as she opened the oven door and violently prodded the roast again.

"Well, this is going to be a nice family meal. I don't want anything to ruin it. Set the table, please."

The dining room was paneled in dark wood, and held a large oak table and an old-fashioned meat safe that served as a sideboard. The chairs were odd, a collection harvested from antique shops in country Tasmania over many years of family excursions. Each one signified an uncomfortable trip in the family car in which the backseat was shared by the three boys and an oak chair carefully arranged on top of them.

Trout fetched the placemats and the boxed cutlery from the meat safe.

"Soup spoons!" his mother called out, and he laid out the soup spoons along with the knives and forks. His mother brought in a basket of rolls.

"Can you gather everyone up? And nicely, please. Don't just stand at the bottom of the stairs and yell."

Trout found his father and Dan hiding in the lounge room. Mrs. M and her nice family meals were an awesome force of nature.

"Where's Richard?" he asked his father.

"Went out to visit some girl," Mr. M said, and winked at Dan.

Dan rolled his eyes.

"Up in his room, I think," Dan said. "I'll get him."

Mrs. M appeared in the doorway. "Dan, come and help me serve up."

"But . . ."

Mrs. M raised her eyebrows and Trout went upstairs to fetch Richard.

"Lunch is ready," Trout said to Richard's bedroom door.

Richard opened the door. Trout didn't notice that he looked grayish and worn out.

"Trout. Let's talk?"

"Lunch is ready," Trout repeated by way of an answer.

"Do you have to be like this?"

"No," said Trout, threateningly. "I don't have to be like *this*."

Richard shook his head and went to push past him.

Trout shoved Richard's shoulder. "Why couldn't you leave her alone?"

"I just . . . I just . . ." Richard struggled for a way of explaining it. "I couldn't. I mean, what's with her? It's not . . . natural."

There was something in Richard's voice that Trout couldn't bear to hear. Anger? Helplessness? "You could have stayed away. You could have. You're just selfish. You always get what you want."

Mrs. M appeared at the bottom of the stairs. "It's on the table," she said, a determined smile fixed onto her face.

"We're just coming," Richard said impatiently, but she stayed and watched them descend the stairs.

Richard tried to speak to Trout again after they'd eaten, but Mrs. Montmorency made Richard help with the washing up so she could have him to herself for a while. Meanwhile, Trout went to his room, fully intending to hide until Richard drove off with Grunt.

CHAPTER FIFTEEN

Undine still fought the occasional wave of nausea sweeping upward from her gut as she stood at the doorway, surveying her bedroom. Now that she was here, she was not sure what to do with herself.

She had come close, really close, to surrendering herself. Not to Richard but to the magic. It hadn't been like the storm this time, which had happened before she even knew it was happening. This time she had almost been in control of it. The sensation had been heady, tempting. For the most transient of moments, she had wanted to transform herself, let the magic change her completely, irrevocably. She'd held Richard, dangled him as if he had been one of Jasper's plastic toys. If she'd wanted to, she could have—

Downstairs, glass tinkled; something had broken. Lou's anger seeped through the floorboards. Undine flopped onto the bed. She looked at the rumpled covers and thought maybe she should just get in. Despite the streaming early afternoon sun there was definitely something tempting about burying herself in her duvet and sleeping for, say, the next five years. But she was restless. The magic was almost totally gone now; however, a faint undertow of it tugged inside her.

She had tried to push the magic away. In the pub the night before, she had pretended, almost successfully, to be a normal girl. Today was proof that there was nothing normal about her.

At the thought, she felt an unexpected thrill of excitement. What she could do, her power, it was . . .

it was *amazing*. It was dangerous: it was the glittering blade of a knife; it was the momentum and single-mindedness of a bullet. It was also vivid and intoxicating. She was almost tempted to use it again, to find Richard and see what would have happened if Lou had not come home.

It was clear that no one here could help her. Not Lou, or Trout, or Richard, or Mim. There was only one person in the whole wide world who could make sense of the last few days of her life, and she had no idea where to find him.

Should she confront Lou, rage, force her to tell her? Beg? Beguile? Did Lou even know? A phone book was no help, Undine didn't even have a name.

Undine, Undine, it's time to come home . . . The voice. The magical manifestations in her room. If it was her father communicating with her, then could it work both ways? Could she find a way to return the call?

She closed her eyes and concentrated on the residual magic she could feel lingering inside her. She imagined it to be a small burning thread. Experimentally, she tried to provoke the flame, tease it into life. Suddenly it sputtered and burst, and the flame arced through her. Undine nearly lost control of it again. She reined it in, with an enormous effort, and tried to make it a soft, friendly, flickering light.

She focused on the voice, tried to find it inside her. There it was, faint but ever present. She tried to locate it outside, in the world, but it was no good. She couldn't focus the magic, couldn't push it in the direction she wanted it to go.

She opened her eyes and sagged, defeated. It was no use. She simply didn't know enough about her power to make it work for her.

But the magic inside her stirred. She watched a hole open up at eye level, a fine rip through the air. She could hear seagulls. She could smell the sea. She felt a fine spray of water on her face. Something—a book—dropped out of the air. Then the schism sealed, and was gone.

It was startling, and yet . . . not. She was not sure

if she had done it, if she'd made it happen, or if it was merely a coincidence. Or if perhaps somehow, her father had known she was trying to contact him and had bridged the gap between them.

She picked up the book, *The Tempest*. The leather cover was brittle, as if the book had been exposed to salt and sand, damp perhaps, or a dry, desiccating heat. It looked like it might fall to pieces in her hands. Carefully she opened the front cover which, as she had feared, cracked. The spine crumbled, and the pages hung loosely, ready to spill onto the floor, each one coarse but frail. She began to close the book but noticed in the corner of the first page, written in elegant curled letters, a name and an address.

Prospero Marine
Bay of Angels
Tasmania

It didn't seem to Undine like an actual address. She couldn't imagine, for example, that she could write it on a postcard and expect the card to arrive anywhere real.

She would like to find the passage again, the one on the scroll of paper from the cigar case. How had it started? Something, something, *thy father lies* . . .

"Whatever," she told herself impatiently. "What about a bloody road map?"

She stood at the top of the stairs, listening for Lou. All was quiet. She quickly located the book of road maps downstairs. Bay of Angels. It was southeast of Hobart, a tiny, remote-looking bay. There was one small road in from the peninsula road, Beach Road, represented by brown dots, indicating it was a dirt road.

Undine felt a surge of excitement. As she stared at the map, another thought occurred to her. She found the phone book and with shaking hands looked up Marine. He was there, the only resident amongst businesses like Marine Construction & Towing Services Pty. Ltd. and Marine Insurance.

As she dialed the number her heartbeat was so

loud in her ears that she thought he might hear it. The phone rang and rang until she was sure it would go unanswered. Her heart nearly broke through her ribcage when someone picked up.

She stood there, holding the receiver. She said nothing; nor did the person who had picked up on the other end. She had the feeling that the person on the other end of the phone was *listening* to her silence, as carefully as he might listen to her speak, and she waited for him to say something. And then he did.

"Undine," said a perfectly ordinary—if slightly shaky—male voice on the other end of the phone. "Undine. It's time to come home."

Part Two

CHAPTER SIXTEEN

Trout lay on his bed, listening to the sound of car doors opening and closing, and Richard's footsteps on the stairs as he ran up for one last thing.

His mother followed behind, chanting the items Richard was expected to take with him, as if she were performing some bizarre ritual or conjuring a spell: "Toothbrush, laundry detergent, soap, phone card, white socks, black socks . . ." The list droned on. Richard, apparently oblivious, clattered back down the stairs.

Trout was nearly asleep in the heat of the afternoon, listening to the rise and fall of the boys' voices as they packed up the car. Then, so close to the edge of sleep that at first he thought he was dreaming, he heard her. Undine. He wanted to get up and look, but he knew the movement of the curtain might catch someone's eye. He sat next to the window, listening to what they were saying.

"So, are you running away?" he heard Richard ask. "Where are you going, anyway?"

Trout heard Undine answer, but couldn't catch the words, just the rising lilt of her voice.

Then Richard again: "Is this about Trout? About us?"

This time Undine's answer was clear. "No. Really. It's complicated. There's been some other stuff going on lately that I can't explain. Family stuff."

So Undine hadn't confided in Richard. It gave Trout a dull sense of satisfaction. Yeah right, he thought. Dull like a dull *knife*, sticking into my *throat*.

Then Grunt was saying, "Is this all you've got?"

and they were gone. As he heard the car rev up the street, he couldn't help but look out the window. It seemed so unlikely, but there was Undine, in the backseat. And he had no idea where she was going! How would he find her?

He felt anger rising. "Why do you *want* to find her?" he asked aloud. "Let *Richard* find her." Though of course, *Richard* already knew where she was going. He kicked his bed petulantly and stubbed his toe, bringing tears to his eyes.

His toe throbbed. He rubbed it absentmindedly, still preoccupied with thoughts of Undine. Was she on a wild goose chase, searching for answers that didn't exist? Was she running to something, or away from something? Either way she might get hurt, and she was alone. Richard didn't count. He was sure Richard didn't have a clue about the danger Undine might be in. He hadn't seen the storm spilling out of her, or the way it almost crushed her.

"Forget about it," he instructed himself sternly.

"It's not your problem anymore," he said two hours later, as he struggled with his physics textbook.

"She doesn't even want to be found," he told his reflection in the microwave as he waited for his meal of leftovers to reheat, while Mrs. M lay down in her room to recover from their nice family meal.

"Even if she did," he mused to his upside-down self in the teaspoon after he'd sucked off the Ovaltine, "she wouldn't want to be found by you . . ."

Undine, he pondered, Undine . . . where would you go? His eyes came to rest on yesterday's newspaper, and he stared at the headline for some time before he was able to take in what it was saying: FREAK STORM CATCHES WEATHER WATCHERS BY SURPRISE. He read the article twice and then pushed the newspaper away. Where had she gone? How could he find out? He squinted blearily at the paper.

He died before you were born. . . . That's what Lou had told Undine about her father. But Trout was sure that wasn't true. He still had that quote from *The Tempest* and he'd read it over and over. He was convinced it meant that Undine's father was somewhere alive, trying to communicate with his daughter. Which meant Lou had lied to Undine, all her life.

He shut his physics book with a satisfyingly loud clap. "Head," he addressed his swirling brain sternly. "Shut up."

He opened his textbook again and began to read, but even physics made less sense now that he'd seen Undine produce a storm out of nothing. Actually, science in general suddenly seemed on wobbly ground.

Usually Trout found patterns of numbers comforting. Once he began calculating equations he would find himself transported to the same place, he imagined, where artists went when they painted, or musicians when they played. But today, he stayed firmly where he was, trapped inside his disappointing self.

He was flicking restlessly through his physics

book when his eye rested for a moment on the chapter heading for chaos theory. He remembered his idea—the one he'd had a million years ago, the night Undine turned into a girl who could make a storm—that Undine's magic might have been like chaos theory. The butterfly effect: a butterfly flaps its wings in Japan and causes a storm in North America a few weeks later. . . . Perhaps instead of making a whole storm, Undine had simply made the right butterfly somewhere flap its wings. At least then she would be using energy that already existed, because it made no sense that energy could come from nowhere.

His dad came in. "You going to digest that, son?" Trout realized he was gnawing on his pencil.

"Can I use your computer, Dad?"

"Games?" Trout wasn't allowed his own computer. Something to do with spending eleven hours straight playing Doom in Year 6. Undine had said, "I'm sure it's a good thing. Give you your own computer and within a week you'd be taking over the world."

Trout told the truth. "Research." He didn't have to say what he was researching. His dad shrugged (which meant yes) and reached for the coffee plunger.

Trout hadn't been the first to put the concepts of chaos theory and magic together. There were sites plastered all over cyberspace, some of them highly theoretical and almost incomprehensible and some mind-bogglingly insipid: "How to perform a simple glamor. This spell will change your eye color. (Note, you will not be able to see the difference, nor will anyone else.)" "Well, *duh!*" Trout said out loud. What he couldn't find, though, was anything about real magic, the magic he had witnessed, the kind Undine was capable of.

He noticed that one of the sites about magic and science had a chat facility. Looking at the stats he could see it was a pretty active site, with several members currently online. He sighed. He thought it was worth a go, though online chatting made him nervous. It was like going to a party where you didn't know anyone—worse, because there were no cheese puffs! What if no one talked to you? What if even computer nerds thought you weren't cool enough?

He signed in, and entered a room called Magick and the Chaosphere and posted his query.

TROUT: I'm trying to find info about chaos magic. Can anyone help me?
MAX: What info?
hookgirl: fishy! here fishy fishy fishy . . .
iceWitch: Not another teenwitch!
MagicMan2000: No love potions here.
hookgirl: come and play fishy fishy . . . o . . . o . . . o
TROUT: Not playing. Important.

A new window popped up. It was a private message from the poster called Max.

● ● ●

MAX: Just ignore those cyberpunk losers. They don't know anything about magic. Last year they were Satanists. Next year *shrug*

TROUT: Can you help me?

MAX: What you want to know??

TROUT: What is chaos magic?

MAX: ?? Impossible to say. It resists definition.

TROUT: What are the rules? The laws?

MAX: No rules. No laws.

TROUT: But what does a chaos magician do? Is it real magic?

MAX: Why you want to know??

TROUT: For a friend. Please. It's really important.

There was a pause. Trout wondered if Max was still online. But it became clear that Max was simply gathering his thoughts.

MAX: How does the universe work? How did the universe come to exist? We used to answer these questions with a simple answer: God. But the

Greeks knew that the universe was born of chaos. Now scientists know too. The Big Bang. Order from chaos. The dictionary defines chaos as: utter confusion or disorder, wholly without organization or order. But chaos theory is equally concerned with order as it is with chaos. Do you know what chaos theory is?

TROUT: Patterns of order that can be found in apparently disordered systems. Like in the weather.

MAX: Yes! But not just the weather. The patterns of Saturn's rings, heart attacks . . .

TROUT: But that's science. What about magic?

MAX: Not finished. More background. Be good. :)

TROUT: LOL. Sorry. Go on.

MAX: Chaos magic is kind of postmodern magic. It doesn't accept basic truths. Religion, science, occultism . . .

TROUT: I'm not sure I understand postmodernism.

MAX: TROUT, no one understands postmodernism! LOL. Anyway, basically if you were into Wicca, you'd have to perform rites, rituals, invoke the

Goddess, that sort of thing. That kind of magic is based on a system of beliefs but chaos magic = no rituals. No beliefs. It just is.

TROUT: So anyone can be a chaos magician?

MAX: That's what those cyberpunks would like to think. But to tell you the truth, no. I get it. I understand all the theory but I've never been able to make magic happen. In fact, I don't know anyone who has.

Trout's fingers hesitated over the keys. He was so tempted to tell Max everything, but how did he know if he could be trusted? Max could be anyone . . . but so, Trout reflected, could Trout. The Internet gave Trout anonymity—there was no way Max could figure out Trout's, or Undine's, real identity.

The decision was made for him. "Come on, mate." His dad stood in the doorway. "That doesn't look like research to me. Don't let your mum catch you."

"Yep," said Trout and wrote *Gotta go*. He book-marked the site before logging off. But even as he watched the flash of blue on the last screen as the computer shut down, he knew that he was going to confide in Max. He needed a friend. He needed whatever he could get.

CHAPTER SEVENTEEN

The house on Beach Road had once been painted a bright buttery yellow. The color had faded with the weather, and sea salt had eroded the paint, so that it flaked off in large pieces. Yet the house still managed to look cheerful despite its weatherworn appearance, sitting upright in its overgrown garden, tucked off the road. From the road the house looked deserted, so still and quiet it was hard to imagine it had ever known human occupation.

As she drew closer though, Undine heard the

chime of a clock from somewhere inside. It was a relief to know that time moved inside the house in the same way it did out here, because she could easily have convinced herself otherwise.

She wished now that she had asked Richard to stay with her. Grunt had offered but it wasn't Grunt she wanted. Richard had refused to meet her eye. Undine didn't have the expertise required to melt the frosty air between them. So she had feigned confidence and sent them away, extracting a promise from Richard that he would not tell Trout or anyone where she was. He had given it indifferently, as if he didn't really care what became of her.

"Well, bye," she said, and her voice sounded forlorn, even to her own ears, so much so that for a moment Richard softened. He reached his hand through the open window and squeezed her arm good-bye.

Grunt had sped off, the wheels of the Fiat spinning on the gravel road, leaving a long skid mark and a whirl of dust behind him.

Undine felt she might have underestimated Grunt at the pub. He had kept up a steady stream of cheery banter as they drove through the city, almost disguising the awkwardness between Undine and Richard.

They drove past the markets, past the docks and the botanical gardens and Government House, over the arching bridge that spanned the Derwent. They continued down the highway that bypassed Hobart's eastern suburbs. Undine watched as the suburbs became farther and farther apart, separated by tracts of countryside, until they were passing through what were more like towns than suburbs.

They had been driving for less than an hour, but they stopped for coffee and doughnuts in Sorell and ate by the side of the road, leaning against the car.

Undine felt hyperaware of Richard beside her. She would only have had to extend her little finger to brush his skin, yet it was as if there was an unfathomable distance between them, a distance that she had no talent to fill.

Part of her wanted to touch him or have him

touch her, take her hand, kiss her, and say beautiful things. But then he moved slightly, and she felt herself pull back, so abruptly it was impossible for him not to have noticed. His face was unreadable. He screwed the paper bag into a tight ball and stuffed it inside his empty polystyrene cup.

Thinking about Richard made her twitchy; thinking about her destination made it ten times worse. Undine followed their progress on the map and, as they drew closer, felt her stomach seize with nervousness. She almost asked Grunt to turn around and drive her back to the city.

Grunt twisted in his seat to look at her every time he talked to her. "Are you okay?" he asked her eventually. "You look kind of pale."

"I'm okay. Just a little carsick," she lied.

Grunt slowed the car and pulled over. "Sit in the front, Undine. Wind the window down for her, Richard, and then get in the back."

Richard did as he was told, and Undine climbed sheepishly into the front seat.

The road unspooled ahead, black as molasses, slick and new, shimmery with sunlight. At the edges it crumbled away, new into old, gravel and blue metal scattering into dirt and scrub. Puddles formed just over the rise and then dissolved, mirages, magical tricks of the light. On the side of the road lay a whole dead bird—a seagull, its torn feathers teased by the wind. Undine watched as they approached the bird. For a moment they seemed to hover in the air, time stopped as she contemplated its still form. Then the moment was gone and they whizzed past; she craned her head back and watched until they disappeared around a bend in the road, and it was forgotten forever.

With the window open she could smell the sea. Most of the time it was a fresh, salty, ever-so-faintly fishy smell, similar to the smell in her bedroom the last few mornings. But sometimes, when they were driving past inlets of stagnant water or sheltered coves where seaweed was gathered in huge mounds on the beaches, the smell was almost unbearably strong, seaweedy and fishy, like tinned anchovies, but also sulphuric, like bad eggs.

Eventually they reached the turnoff to Bay of Angels. It was marked with a small white sign, the paint blistered with age.

Undine consulted the map. "You can just let me off here if you like," she said. "It's not far to walk."

But Grunt had already made the turn and was driving down the deteriorating road.

Fifteen minutes later, they turned right on a road that was equal parts sand and gravel, which was, they all agreed, Beach Road, though there was no street sign, and the water could only just be glimpsed through the thick scrub.

It was not hard to find what they were looking for. When the house came into view, Undine had a glimmer of déjà vu. She *recognized* it, as clearly as she would have recognized her own house if she were returning to it after a long and difficult journey. Besides, on the mailbox, written in thick, wobbly black letters, was the name Prospero Marine.

Undine stared out the window of the car at the tattered yellow house. Yellow like butter, yellow like daffodils. Less yellow than the highlighter pen she had used to mark passages of *The Iliad*. More yellow than her student copy of *Hamlet*.

"Cool name. Weird. Who is he?" Grunt had asked.

Undine had answered, still in a dream. "My father."

There was no sign of him. Undine realized that he wasn't necessarily expecting her. She looked up at the road where Grunt and Richard had been only minutes before. She half hoped they would come back, tell her it had all been some terrible mistake, that they had met a Prospero Marine on his way to buy the paper—or some other profoundly normal activity—and he hadn't been the one she was looking for at all.

She continued walking around the house, giving it a wide berth, reluctant to knock on the door.

"Yeah, good," she told herself. "Come all this way and *then* change your mind."

The garden was enormous, and filled with a strange collection of things: fat roses and fatter hydrangeas, fuchsias with pink flowers and hard dark purple pods, a peppercorn tree, lemon trees, a peach tree. From hanging baskets on the veranda grew long tendriling succulents, bright green, full of new growth. Late-flowering jasmine was entwined around the beams of the veranda and clung to the lip of the roof. Raspberry canes were bursting with fruit in one sheltered corner of the garden. Sunflowers were everywhere, displaying vivid auras of yellow petals to match the house.

In places where the soil was sandy, and dry, spindly plants of a grayish blue color grew; small and mean-looking, but hardy, they were probably natives, products of the harsh environment. Beyond the garden there were gum trees, bent and twisted by the wind. There were also a number of prickled, scrubby bushes: more natives, adapted to the salt air and eroded soil.

Against that backdrop, the garden looked even more unlikely. It must have taken some work to make this garden productive; it was almost against nature for plants to flourish here.

It was so quiet. It felt otherworldly, peaceful, and yet underneath it there was something else, a kind of buzzing. When she concentrated on it, it became higher pitched and filled her head with noise, or noiselessness. White noise, Trout would call it. It was more like vibration than noise, like movement, currents in the air. But it was not dissimilar to the voice she had lived with for the past days.

She saw a glimmer of movement and jumped, then felt foolish. It was a cat, a long low sleek thing, emerging from the rhododendron. As it turned its tail to her it looked odd and lumpy. Pregnant, she thought. She held her hand out to the cat but it ignored her. She followed the cat around to the back of the house, where it slithered into a space under the veranda. There was a back door, at which sat two large Wellington boots. The first sign of human habitation, they made Undine uneasy, as if they could conjure Prospero from his booted feet up.

She turned away from the house, telling herself off for being a wimp. It was then that she noticed the narrow sandy path leading through the grassy dunes toward the sea, and all at once it was as if she'd always known it was there.

She left her own shoes and bag by the Wellingtons, and walked along the sandy path barefoot. She climbed over the rise, and it was from this high vantage point that she saw properly—for the first time in her life—the sea.

It made the river, the only other expanse of water she had known, seem listless and dull in comparison. This was the buzzing she had heard, this was the vibration in the air, but here it was a thousandfold. The drumming of the sea, the awesome power of the waves. They were huge, and each one seemed to have a colossal life of its own. Or the sea itself was like an animal, the waves its wild, primal language. The gusty wind that blew in from the water seemed to be a product of the sea, generated from the force of the waves.

She felt energy coursing through her and knew this: some part of her—the secret, dangerous part—was home. This was where her magical self belonged. It was as if she was feeling the storm pass through her, as it had that night, but all at once and only for a moment. The outside world remained unaffected. The sensation was not unpleasant; she was filled with adrenaline and her heart raced.

It excited her to realize that she might learn how to control the magic, how to *use* it. It was a new and powerful idea, that this immense magic could become part of her life, seamlessly bonded to her, something not to fight but to embrace.

The beach was an extended half-moon shape, covered in dull yellow sand. It curled around so that nothing could be seen at either point but the high cliffs that encircled it. About a kilometer out to sea from the shore stood tall columns of rock, four of them, jutting out of the water. They looked smooth and bright, and the sun drew out a rosy, golden hue from the stone. Undine guessed these were the "angels" after which the Bay was named.

And far beyond the angels the sea stretched to the fine, far-off line of the horizon, beyond which there was apparently nothing. This was where the world curved away from her, Undine thought, toward distant foreign places.

There was a man at the far end of the beach, walking with some difficulty but nonetheless making rapid progress. She could not discern any detail of his appearance from where she stood, except that he had on a flapping coat that fluttered in the wind like a sail, and to Undine it seemed that this somehow contributed to his quick pace. He had a dog with him, a large brown one with a wonky gait, which was running up the beach in her direction, churning sand under its paws, barking happily.

She slid down the dune and, with a deep breath, walked up to meet them.

CHAPTER EIGHTEEN

On *the beach,* the dog reached her first, greeting Undine as though she were an old friend, leaping up to rest its paws on Undine's shoulders, tail wagging ceaselessly.

The dog turned and loped back up the beach to Prospero, and then returned to Undine, looking up brightly and encouragingly at her face, as if it were formally introducing them.

They stood for a moment, looking at each other.

"Undine," Prospero said. "Welcome home."

Prospero Marine's face was craggy and worn; years of wind, salt, and sun had weathered him, as it had weathered the house in which he lived. He seemed very old—too old to be the father of a teenage girl. His body was crooked; his voice shook. His left eye was motionless and a vivid, translucent blue. The other eye, though paler and a grainy gray, glittered and traveled effortlessly to and fro, exploring its surroundings as though it were living, sentient.

That eye, the glittering one, frightened Undine, though the other lifeless one appeared more immediately unsettling. It seemed to see everything, to see deep inside her, scrutinizing and inscrutable.

Prospero said, "And how was your trip?" as though everything about this meeting were ordinary. "What do you think of my bay?" he added.

Undine looked out at the enormous waves. "It seems . . . familiar."

"Well, of course, you were born here," Prospero said. "And my family has always drawn their livelihoods from the sea—fishing, harvesting salt and kelp. There's seawater in your blood." Fleetingly, Undine wondered if he meant literally.

"The angels are beautiful," she said.

"We can walk right out to the closest one, there," Prospero pointed, "at low tide."

Undine smiled weakly, made shy by Prospero's self-assurance.

They did not speak of the circumstances of their meeting, nor did Prospero ask how she had found him. As they reached the path to the house, the dog ran ahead into the garden. It collapsed under the shade of a large peppercorn tree, panting.

Prospero held the back door open for her. "Tea?" After the long, glowing light of the setting evening sun, the darkness of the house seemed to swallow him. Undine inhaled deeply and followed him inside.

They sat at a Laminex table in the kitchen of the yellow house. Undine played with the anodized aluminum sugar bowl, which was cherry red like the table. The benches were laminated in a groovy, vivid green, and the cupboards were dark wood veneer with red handles. There were red tiles on the walls, between the cupboards and the benches. Even the taps in the kitchen sink were red. It was like a time warp. Mim would love this kitchen, Undine thought. Mim would *die* over this kitchen.

It was a reminder of her promise to Mim. Perhaps Undine should have told Mim where she was going. But Mim would have told Lou—how couldn't she? Mim would have felt responsible. No, it was better that Mim didn't know. Still, Undine couldn't shake off the feeling that she had let Mim down, by making a promise that she couldn't keep.

But Mim was a world away and belonged to some other part of Undine. Undine was here now, and she had so many questions for Prospero that she couldn't frame just one.

Undine didn't realize she was spinning the sugar bowl around and around on the table until Prospero reached out his hand and held it still. For a moment his fingers brushed hers. She expected something magical, a jolt like the electricity of the storm, but all she felt was the warmth of his skin. Her skin stayed warm as his hand left hers. There was a sudden pressure of tears against her eyes, though she did not cry. This was her *father*. But what did that mean?

Ask him, she urged herself. But she couldn't make the words come out. He had not mentioned anything about the magic, and she found neither could she. She wondered what he was feeling. Was he pleased to see her? Excited to know her? Did he see some vestige of himself in her? Did he see Lou?

"I'll show you where you can put your things."

Undine followed him down the hallway. He gestured at each room as they passed it. "The living room. The bathroom. Toilet's on your left. My bedroom; my study is the annex off this room. The corner room, which was your mother's. It's still full of her things, I've never got round to clearing it out. And here. This is your room."

The last room was small but cozy, painted the

same daffodil yellow as the exterior walls. It was furnished as a nursery, with a handmade wooden crib by the windows, veiled with a mosquito net. There was also a low, fold-out single bed, neatly made up, as if he'd been expecting her.

"Lou made the crib. It was yours, of course."

Undine ran her hand over the textured wood of the crib. Lou had never made a thing in all the time Undine had known her. The crib was beautiful, wild and organic, as though it had been cobbled together from living branches. It released a faint woody odor, like resin.

Prospero gazed at her smooth hand resting on the crib. He seemed such an old man, so powerless. And yet she felt sure that once he had *surged* with power; there was a dignity about him that hinted at a stronger man, as though his past, young self was trapped inside a cage of old bones, yellowed teeth, and loose skin.

"We haven't . . . I mean, I . . . I don't know if I'm staying." Undine looked at her hands while she spoke. Her nails badly needed a trim and a good scrubbing.

"Well, you just make up your mind when you're ready. Only, I don't know how you're going to get back up to town. The buses don't come down to the Bay. And I don't run a car. Do you have your license?"

Undine shook her head.

"I suppose you could always ring your mother, ask her to come and pick you up."

"No," said Undine quickly.

Prospero raised his eyebrows.

"No," Undine began again, keeping her voice steady. "I think I'd like to stay. At least for tonight. We *do* have a lot to talk about."

"Indeed we do," he agreed, holding her gaze effortlessly, and Undine noticed that his left eye was not as bad as she first thought. It seemed to have some small movement in it after all.

A vicious squawking resounded through the house.

"Ah yes," Prospero said cheerfully, "Caliban."

Undine followed him down the dimly lit internal hallway, which smelled faintly of dog hair and carpet shampoo.

In a large bell-shaped cage in the living room was an oversized parrot that looked as if it had seen better days. It cocked its head and caught Undine's eye, bobbing up and down, laughing at her.

"Does it speak?" Undine asked, charmed.

"Who's a pretty bird then?" Prospero asked the unattractive bird.

The bird released a stream of invective that would have made even the most hardened school-bus driver blush.

" 'You taught me language, and my profit on't is I know how to curse.' "

Undine looked questioningly at her father.

"Act one, scene two," Prospero said.

She shook her head, still mystified.

"Have you not actually read *The Tempest*?" her father asked, dismayed.

"Um, no. I haven't quite got around to it yet . . . I brought it with me," Undine added defensively.

"What sort of education do they give you these days?"

"We did *Hamlet* at school," Undine offered apologetically.

Prospero made a deep grumbling sound. "But my note. 'Full fathom five thy father lies . . .'" he intoned. "Don't tell me it had no dramatic effect whatsoever."

"Oh yes, absolutely," Undine assured him. "I had a good interpreter."

With sudden physical pain she wished Trout were there. Prospero raised his thick eyebrows and Undine wondered if they were what books meant when they said beetling. If Trout *was* here, she thought abstractedly, he would know what a beetling eyebrow was.

CHAPTER NINETEEN

Undine sat on the bed, listening to the sound of Prospero making dinner in the kitchen. The day was beginning to lose color outside, though there were still a few hours before dark. She felt a twinge of homesickness, wondering if Lou was missing her yet. Jasper would be eating his tea now. She missed his face, even though it was not that long since she'd seen him.

Outside, the dog barked. Undine heard a car pull up. She heard Prospero muttering in the hallway, "All right, all right, no need to shout, Ariel. You needn't sound so bloody happy about it."

From her window she couldn't see the road. She couldn't imagine Prospero having visitors, but presumed he must. Without a car he would at least need his groceries delivered. Unless he just magicked them up out of the air. Tinned tomatoes and magic beans, using his power for the good of his colon.

Her thoughts returned to the car and she felt a sudden burst of excitement. Maybe it was Richard! Maybe he had come to see her, to apologize for his surly behavior on the journey down. She felt a surge of longing to feel his fingers on her face. Her stomach twisted with nerves. Of course it was Richard. Who else knew she was here? And it had been so close, they had almost . . . He *was* her boyfriend, wasn't he?

She had so convinced herself that she was surprised to open the door and find Grunt sitting on the steps of the veranda, talking to Prospero.

"Hey," Grunt said, looking a bit shy. "I had to get

some supplies, so I thought I'd drop in to make sure you're okay."

"I'm fine," said Undine. Her voice rang with disappointment and she cringed to hear it.

Ariel assaulted Grunt with kindness. Grunt was trying to pat her and fend her off at the same time, though it seemed to be a losing battle.

"Your dad's been telling me about the wreck in the Bay," Grunt said, turning his head to one side to avoid getting a mouthful of dog. "I thought I might come back tomorrow and have a dive. We aren't starting work until Monday, and I'm keener on marine archaeology anyway. That's if it's okay with you, of course."

"Yeah, no, that's fine," said Undine, feeling a bit bewildered. "Um, what wreck in the Bay?"

Prospero beamed. "The *Babylon*. She went down in the 1890s. A cargo ship: slate, timber, copper, wool."

"Oh." She remembered her dream: the wrecked ships, the drowned sailors, her dress weighted with stones. She thought about the Bay, picturing the seabed littered with human bones, and shivered.

Grunt tipped his head back and finished his tea with a gulp.

"You might as well have a look at the Bay. While you're here," said Prospero. "Undine will show you while I make us some dinner. Would you like to stay, Alastair?"

Grunt hesitated. "No, thanks," he said reluctantly. "They're expecting me back."

As they walked to the beach, Undine asked, "Why do they call you Grunt if your name is Alastair? I guessed it was a nickname for Grant."

"I got stuck with Grunt in high school. I was pretty monosyllabic back then. Everyone thought I was a bit thick."

"But you're not!" It was a statement not a question.

Grunt smiled easily. "I played a lot of sports, and fell over a lot. Got bumped on the head all the time. Then I broke my leg and had to sit still for six weeks. Started reading. Was bored enough to do my homework. Turned out I wasn't so dumb after all. Mum banned me from rugby after that. She thought it was a miracle."

Undine looked at him sideways, trying to work out if he was pulling her leg or not. "Truly?" she asked him.

His face revealed nothing, though his eyes seemed to have an extra sparkle in them.

"So why did you really come?" she asked him.

"I just . . . had a feeling, that's all," Grunt replied. "I guessed you didn't know your dad too well."

"This is actually the first time I've met him. My mother told me . . ." Undine broke off, instinctively loyal to Lou. "My mother wasn't exactly truthful," she amended, lamely.

"My parents divorced when I was twelve," Grunt told her. "It kind of broke my dad's heart. He moved to Launceston, where all broken-hearted people go." He smiled wryly and Undine imagined the small, shabby city filled with desolate people, injured by love. "He just kind of died inside. I don't see him much. I think I remind him, you know, of my mum. He loves me. But it hurts him."

"That's sad."

"Yeah. So how's it going so far?"

"I don't know. Different, I suppose, from what I expected. Though I don't know exactly what I expected. I guess I thought that everything would suddenly make sense. That all the pieces of my life would fall into place, that I would suddenly *know* myself."

Grunt, standing at the high point of the path, looked out over the angels, which glistened in the last rays of the setting sun. The sun also caught his dreadlocks, making his coarse white-blond hair luminous.

"Wow," he said. "They're awesome. I can't believe I never knew about this place. I grew up near here," he added, "Back up the coast, toward Dunalley." He pointed to the farthest angel. "Your dad says that's where the *Babylon* went down. He's taking me out on his boat tomorrow. He said at low tide you can see it clearly from the surface."

Undine followed the direction of his pointing finger, looking out at the bay. The sea still seemed to hum inside her. She felt it must be patently obvious, this extraordinary effect the sea had on her. Looking down to avoid his eyes, she saw a huge, sweeping circle in the sand and in it more circles, jumbled together, circles inside circles until the last one was just a smudgy smear.

She caught her breath.

"Wow," said Grunt. "Check out that sand formation! Must be the wind or something. I've never seen anything like it."

"Mmm," said Undine, deliberately vague. All things considered, she doubted it was a natural phenomenon, but some trick of Prospero's, a gesture of his talent.

"You're not easily impressed!" Grunt joked.

Undine walked him back up to the car. "See you tomorrow," she said.

"Maybe," Grunt said. "Depends what time you get up. It'll be early."

Grunt pulled his hand through his thick dread-locks. They looked coarse and stiff, affected perhaps by sun and salt water. She had a sudden urge to touch them, to see if they felt as bristly as they looked. She clasped her hands behind her back and asked quickly, "Will Richard come?"

"I don't think so. He . . ."

"It's all right," she said, more sharply than she intended. "He doesn't have to come if he doesn't want to."

Grunt raised his eyebrows, but not unkindly. "Well, see you tomorrow," he said. Undine nodded tightly, but as Grunt drove off she relented and raised her hand to wave good-bye.

Prospero had poached a fish for tea, dressed with a dill sauce and accompanied by roasted new potatoes and French beans. Undine had to admit to herself she was surprised. She'd expected bachelor food: tins of things, like sardines and baked beans and soup, and hastily rinsed dishes instead of carefully washed ones, and not enough green vegetables.

Like Stephen, she thought wryly. When they had first met him both Undine and Lou had decided almost straightaway that he was lovely. Later Lou wailed, "But he's *hopeless* in the kitchen!"

Being with Prospero was doing strange things to Undine. She couldn't help but compare him to Stephen, bringing back the raw, acute pain of losing him. And yet in some way she felt hopeful that the memories of Stephen could be . . . not replaced . . . just *eased* somehow by a relationship with this new, old father.

But, she reminded herself, she wasn't here for mushy reunions. Information. That was what she was really after, wasn't it? Why was she too shy to ask?

They ate in silence. Every now and then from the living room Caliban let forth a flurry of "language," which Prospero stoutly ignored.

Now or never, Undine told herself. "Prospero?" she blurted, her fork poised in the air.

Prospero looked at her.

"What am I? The things I can do? What are you?"

Prospero placed his knife and fork carefully on his plate and contemplated her thoughtfully. She held her breath, waiting for his response. She was suddenly terrified of his answer. He resumed eating.

"Finish your dinner. We'll talk after."

Undine had to be satisfied with that. She ate her meal in silence.

CHAPTER TWENTY

The phone and the doorbell rang at the same time.

Trout rushed to the phone but Mrs. M was standing right next to it.

"Hello? Richard! How are you settling in? Are you warm enough? Do you have enough to eat?"

Trout hovered at her, making what he thought to be urgent gestures to let him speak, but after asking Richard a barrage of questions pertaining to food, sleep, and daily ablutions, she hung up the phone.

"What?" said Mrs. M impatiently. "Don't be silly.

He had to go. You'll have a chance to speak with him next time. I don't know," she added. "I can't keep up with you kids. You wouldn't even talk to Richard yesterday."

Mr. M said from in front of the evening news, "Isn't anyone going to answer the bloody door?"

"'Cause you can't possibly do it," Trout grumbled. He sighed theatrically, "*I'll* do it."

Trout was decidedly put out by the sight of Lou on the doorstep. It was like two completely separate elements of his world had collided (much like seeing Undine with Richard).

"Where is she, Trout?" Lou asked straightaway.

"She's not here," Trout replied. "See ya." He went to shut the door in her face. After all, it was partly her fault that Undine had run away: her lies, or half-truths, or withholding of the truth. And Lou had started that stupid fight. While he *sat* there like an *idiot*. It served her right.

But Mrs. M had appeared by Trout's side. She held the door open. "Louise," she said with a nod.

Trout knew that his mother, though always impeccably polite, was never going to be president or treasurer of the Louise Connelly fan club. But when it came to running away, the sisterhood of motherhood (*whatever . . .* he knew what he meant) would win out.

"Undine's gone," Lou said unhappily. "Isn't she here?"

"Trout. If you know where Undine is, you must tell us."

Trout turned reluctantly. "I *don't* know, Mum," he said honestly.

Lou's shoulders sagged and her eyes filled with tears. It was how Trout imagined a volcano might look in slow motion, the solidness and permanence of a mountain melting away. It alarmed him.

"I'm sorry," Trout said, distressed. "I really am sorry. But we sort of . . . we'd had a fight. Or, not exactly, but I was angry with her. I wasn't speaking to her. She didn't tell me anything."

"You don't even know where she might have gone?" Mrs. M pushed. "She's very naughty, worrying Lou like this. Can you think of anywhere she would go?"

Lou spoke, her voice trembly. "Please, Trout. I'm so worried. We've been fighting too. I was *horrible* to her, I said *awful* things."

Mrs. M managed to bring Lou inside and herd a very reluctant Trout at the same time, so they all ended up in the kitchen.

"Now let's see," Trout's mother said matter-of-factly. "She was on the outs with both of you. Maybe she has run away, to scare you perhaps. What do you think, Trout?"

Trout sat at the table, shrinking into his chair like a deflating balloon. "I don't know about running away. I don't think that's it exactly. I don't know. But I know who does."

Both Mrs. M and Lou waited, the question on their faces.

"Can you ring Richard? Do you have a number for him?"

Mrs. M looked confused. "Richard? No." She

explained to Lou: "They're camping." She turned back to Trout. "You don't think she's with Richard, do you?" she asked him.

"No. But I think he knows where she is." Trout suddenly remembered. "What about Grunt's—I mean, Alastair's—mobile?"

Mrs. M nodded and left the room to find the number. She returned carrying the cordless phone. "The recorded message said his phone was switched off or out of range, but I was able to leave a message."

Lou looked crumpled and forlorn, like Jasper when he'd just woken up. "So I have to wait?" she asked, as though it was the hardest thing she could do. Trout was surprised. She always seemed so strong, so self-contained. Now she looked as if she'd been disassembled and put back together, but with some of the important pieces left out. Mrs. M put a cup of tea down in front of her and patted her shoulder. She took another cup out to her husband.

When she left the room, Trout tried to conceal his awkwardness at Lou's fragility. Wanting to offer some comfort, he said, "I think Undine is okay. I'm sure of it."

But Lou leaned forward, almost spilling her tea, and there was a sudden change of climate in her gray-blue eyes. Lightning flashed. In a low voice so Trout's mother wouldn't hear, she said bitterly, "There are things, Trout, that you will never, never understand. So you won't mind if I don't take your word for it. Because Undine is mine. And it is possible that she will never be *okay* again."

Mosquitoes droned in Undine's ear. The moon was a full, fat golden globe in the sky. Through the boards of the veranda, she could see the glinting, slitted eyes of the cat she had followed that morning. It sat poised, listening to Prospero's and Undine's voices vibrating through the wooden floor.

"It's as if"—Undine was trying to explain how she felt about her newfound abilities—"I'm this thing, right? I'm a *thing*, like a key or a cup or a lake. Something someone's laid aside for a while. Forgotten about. And no one told me, because you don't tell a key what it is for, or a lake."

"A thing?" Prospero asked. He repeated incredulously, "A *key*?"

"Yeah." Undine was warming to her analogy. "A key. I'm meant to open something. To *do* something. But no one told me. Because you don't tell a key what it's for. It just *is*. Or does, I suppose. And so I just . . . sit about . . . on a table, or under a rock somewhere—"

"Under a rock?"

"You know, like a spare front door key. Or under the mat or whatever. The rock isn't important."

"But the key is?"

Undine looked at Prospero, frustrated. "Yes," she said slowly, as if Prospero were a small child.

"Daughter," Prospero addressed her, looking out from under his thick eyebrows, "I have no idea what you are talking about."

"The magic."

"Yes," agreed Prospero. "The magic. But where on

earth did you get this idea that you were a *key*?"

"Well!" Undine cried, exasperated. "What *am* I?"

"Powerful," said Prospero. He thought for a minute and added, "Very powerful."

"Am I a witch?"

Prospero laughed, long and deep. "A witch?" he repeated, when his laugh had ended. "Broomsticks and britches? No."

"A sorcerer? A magician?"

Prospero waved his hands about dismissively. "Pick one, if you like. But none of them are really accurate. Sorcerer, magician, wizard, or witch . . . these are all just constructs—myths people have created to enable them to think they have some control over nature. A witch or a sorcerer, they use things, spells and instruments, to exert that control. But in reality, magic isn't a single action. You don't *do* magic. You don't wave a wand. Abracadabra. It's an *event*. Like—let's see—like a supernova. Or a heart attack. You create a whole system of small events—a chain reaction—that

222

makes one big event. It's a very complicated process."

"But you *made* things happen. You deliberately, systematically—"

"Undine. We *are* magic. We're its source and its guide."

Undine frowned. "I don't understand."

Prospero sighed. "Magic isn't just this thing, this *stuff*, hanging about in the universe, waiting to be given a direction. It's generated. It comes from you. From people like you."

"Are there others like us?"

"No one is like you, Undine. You are unique. And the power inside you? It is nothing I've ever dreamed of. It *sings*."

"But there are others, who can do . . . who can be . . . magical?"

Evasively, Prospero answered, "Perhaps one. Or two. It's not merely a human phenomenon. It *can* be connected to an object or a particular physical space. Like here, the Bay. It has its own magic. That's why I stay here. I draw power from it, and so can you."

"And . . . and . . . what do we *do*?"

He answered disapprovingly, as if Undine was asking all the wrong questions. "I'm not sure I understand what you mean by that, Undine."

"Well . . ." Undine was hazy on it herself. "Do we have some kind of . . . job? Sacred duty? Protect the innocent? Fight the good fight? Feed the world?"

Prospero shook his head. "You're still thinking in myths, stories. There's no moral imperative, no agenda. It just . . . *is*."

"Then what's the point of it? Why *us*?"

"There is no why. No point." Prospero sipped his drink and said, sounding for a moment like an ordinary, cantankerous old man, "We don't come with an instruction book, you know."

"I don't understand."

"It's not about what we *should* do. It's about what we *can* do. We have enormous power. We can use it. We can do anything we want. Normal laws, normal rules, don't apply to us."

Undine thought about this. "That sounds . . . lonely."

For the first time Prospero answered uncertainly, as though he was surprised by Undine's observation. Quietly he said, "It can be lonely, I suppose."

Undine asked, "Will you show me?"

"What?"

"Your magic."

"A trick?" Prospero sounded disappointed, as if Undine had failed to grasp some basic concept. "You want me to perform for you?"

Undine could hear a tired whine in her own voice, but she wanted to understand. "Please. I need to see."

Prospero sighed again, but obliged.

At first Undine thought he was going to do something to her, for she felt strange, a queasy dip in her stomach, like being pushed too high on a swing.

But Prospero pointed his right index finger to the sky and moved it in circles. It was the same gesture girls at school made when they thought something was trivial or boring, and so it looked almost comical when Prospero did it, until Undine saw that something was forming at the end of his finger.

It was a small cone of wind, like a miniature tornado. It pulled things into itself, dust and moths and mosquitoes, growing bigger, until Prospero lowered his hand and released it into the garden, where it moved in an elegant figure eight around the lawn. It was like a small animal, something half tame and half wild, in the glowering dusk.

They watched in silence as the small twister curled and spun, dancing across the grass. Eventually, like a child's spinning top, it began to lose momentum, and it slowed, swaying slightly until it finally collapsed, puffing soil and dust into the air and then disappearing.

There was a pause; silence ballooned between them.

"We're not . . . evil, are we?" Undine asked.

Prospero sounded like he was losing his patience. "I told you. Not good. Not evil. We just are."

"Prospero, why am I here? Why now? Why did you call me?"

"Your magic. It sings. For the first time, I could locate you, pinpoint you. The noise of you came together. Isn't it enough. . . ?" His one good eye looked at her directly. "Isn't it enough, that a father should want to see his daughter after so many years?"

She desperately wanted this to be true, for Prospero's motivation to be simple paternal feeling. But why now? Undine thought. Haven't you ever heard of a phone book? She knew there was more to it, that he had some other intention, some other agenda. But if she pushed him now, she might not get the other answers she was seeking.

"And what can I do, exactly?"

"Undine," said Prospero, and his voice was gentler. "You, my dear, can do *anything you want.*"

It was such a typical thing for a father to say to his child, affectionate and normal, yet totally uninformative. Undine felt simultaneously frustrated and absurdly pleased by it. She listened to the drone of crickets while Prospero dozed, his half-full glass tilted at an alarming angle. Gently Undine removed it from his hand and placed it on the boards beside him. The movement roused him.

"Hey," he said, fiercely. "What's that?" He woke properly. "Oh. Time for bed perhaps."

"Yes," Undine agreed. "I think I'll go in." But she didn't move. She needed some time to think about what Prospero had told her. Prospero hadn't really been illuminating—the nature of the magic still eluded her. She suspected the only way of discovering its true nature was to test its power, here in the bay where the magic was strong. The idea terrified her, and thrilled her.

She watched her father raise himself from his chair. As he stood, his age seemed to perceptibly alter. He started in the chair as a very old man, but as he pulled himself upright he appeared to grow rapidly younger, until he was quite a young man, spry and resilient. Then the youth in his face seemed to slide away, and he was old again, and tired. His shoulders drooped as he picked up his glass and shuffled slowly inside.

Trout logged on to the site every chance he got during the day, but Max wasn't around. Finally, after everyone was in bed, Trout logged on again to find Max's name appearing on the left of the screen, indicating that he was online. Trout opened up a private box and messaged him. Picking up straightaway where they had left off, Trout typed, "I know someone who has done real magic." His heart pounded as he waited for Max to respond.

Max appeared.

MAX: Really?

TROUT: She made a storm.

MAX: Your girlfriend?

TROUT: No. I wish. :(

MAX: She really made a storm?

TROUT: Yes. But she didn't mean to. It just kind of happened. I saw it.

MAX: That definitely sounds like chaos magic. I'm jealous!

TROUT: Don't be. It was kind of . . . weird. Big. Scary.

MAX: Yeah! That's the excitement of it. Chaos magic is scary because it's huge. No holds barred. No limitations. Anything can happen.

Max made Undine's magic sound like an extreme sport. What was that thing Dan wanted to do? Base jumping, where you put on a parachute and jump off a cliff. The sort of stupid fun that's fun because you almost die.

MAX: There are limits in traditional magic. You know, there's always a big deal about consequences? Return to the power of three times three and all that, meaning what you get back is worse than what you give out—it's all to do with the balance of the universe. But chaos magicians don't believe in consequences. They believe magic is morally neutral.

• • •

Morally neutral. The term sounded kind of *cold* and dangerous . . . something the military might use, like friendly fire. But there was nothing friendly about being shot. And while the magic might be morally neutral, human beings weren't. No one is above morality.

And, Trout thought, power corrupts.

MAX: Trout? You still there?
TROUT: Yeah, sorry, just thinking.
MAX: You have to tell me more! How did she do it? What else has she done?

Suddenly Trout felt uneasy about the direction the conversation was taking. Nervously, without giving much thought to what he was doing, he moved the cursor over the X in the corner of the private box and jabbed his finger twitchily on the mouse button, ending their chat session.

Of course, it happened all the time in chat rooms—the real world intruded and the session ended abruptly. For all Max knew, Trout was an eleven-year-old boy and his mother had called him downstairs for milk and cookies. But still, as the computer shut down, Trout felt embarrassed. Had he overreacted? It was hard to put his finger on exactly why he had suddenly had to end the session. Oh well, he thought, he could apologize to Max next time.

But as he went through the automatic routine of preparing for bed, washing his face, cleaning his teeth, putting on his pajamas, Trout couldn't shake the feeling that he had made a mistake, discussing Undine with Max.

Undine sat on the veranda looking out at the night. Away from the lights of town, the sky seemed over-crowded with stars, and she looked for the constellations Trout had shown her: the Southern Cross and Orion's belt were easy. In the east she located Sirius, the Dog Star. In the western sky she found Piscis Austrinus, the Southern Fish. She rolled the names around in her mind, remembering the way Trout had whispered them as she peered through the telescope, as if the stars formed the language of incantation.

What would Trout have to say? He had such a scientific mind. Was magic a science? Did it operate within predictable boundaries? Or was it just chaos, an enormous, unruly force spilling out into the universe? Were there really others like Prospero? And like her? Or were they alone?

She looked into the curved dome of the night sky for answers. The universe, Trout had told her, was composed of a very small amount of ordinary matter (like people, plaster, chickens, dust), and a larger quantity of dark matter, but mostly it consisted of dark energy, meaning the universe was expanding at an increasing rate. Undine had never really understood this, but right now it was as if she were watching it accelerate away from her into the infinite blackness.

She looked at the stars. Some of them burned strong and constant, while others, apparently smaller and weaker, occasionally seemed to flicker and go out. Trout would say that what she saw in the night sky didn't represent what was really out there, but instead was a kind of map of the past. The light belonged to stars remote in time and space, some of them old, dead, dark things now. All that light, stored up in the universe . . . photons traveling hundreds of thousands of light years, just to dress the sky in stars.

She wondered, could she rearrange the stars? Was her magic that potent, that it could reorder the universe?

She framed a star with her index finger and her thumb, squinting through at the brave flickering light. She pinched her finger and thumb together and the star disappeared. When she lowered her hand it was still gone, vanished—dark space where the light had once been.

A trick of the night? If she altered a star in the night sky, did that mean she had changed the past? Was this what Prospero felt when he reached out into the air and rearranged the world with his magic—creating infinitesimal vibrations of sound for her ears alone, or small, tame puffs of wind? Something surged through her, breathtaking, and in an instant she recognized what it was.

Power. It was exhilarating.

CHAPTER TWENTY-ONE

Light coming in through a crack in the curtains hit Undine's face and woke her. She had no idea what time it was. She lay in bed listening for telltale sounds, but the house was silent, except for Caliban's occasional squawk.

Despite the astonishing magic of the night before and the extraordinary conversation she'd had with Prospero, she woke up feeling surprisingly mundane. Her bladder was full and her mouth was dry; her eyes felt grainy and leaden.

In the kitchen she found muesli and a clean blue-and-white striped pottery bowl set out on the table, and noticed Prospero's dish draining beside the sink. The clock on the oven said it was just after eight. Prospero was probably the sort to rise early.

She remembered the diving and looked out the kitchen window. The Fiat was parked on the nature strip. They must already be out on the water.

She ate her breakfast; the clink of the spoon hitting the bowl echoed through the empty kitchen. She wondered what Lou and Jasper were doing. She had been away a whole night. Lou would know she was not at Trout's by now. She felt surprisingly gleeful at beating Lou at her own game, and managing to be unpredictable after all. Was Lou missing her?

It was strange thinking about house-on-the-steps-Lou and then remembering that Lou-who-lived-here was the same person. Undine was deeply curious about this other Lou. She pushed her half-eaten breakfast away. She looked carefully out the windows to see if she could spot any sign of Prospero or Grunt and then snuck down the hall. She paused outside Prospero's room. She was dying to get in there, to see what she could find out about her mysterious father. But Caliban screeched and, cowed by his presence, she moved into the slightly less treacherous territory of Lou's old room. Why had Lou had her own room? Undine wondered. Didn't she and Prospero sleep together? Didn't they . . . ? Well, they must have, at least once.

"Ew!" she said, and did a little grossed-out dance trying to get the thought out of her head.

In Lou's old room there was the kind of miscellany that could belong to anyone. Books, blank postcards, pens, cassettes. She rummaged through boxes, but there was nothing there, nothing personal.

She was shoving everything back when from one of the books a small dense nub of paper hit the floor. She unfolded it and smoothed out two pieces of paper. One was a photocopy of an ultrasound print, and looking at the dates she saw it was herself, scooped in a bowl shape, her profile clear and still recognizable as her own.

She recovered the other sheet of paper and found it was a poem, written in Lou's light script. She didn't know Lou wrote poetry. She scanned it quickly.

Ultrasound

A luminous, looping
Scrawl of light.

It's a girl.

She inhabits darkness.
Darkness inhabits her,

Tunneling through a
Dull opening
In her otherwise radiant cranium.

When the moon is said and done,
And the night gives way to dawn

What will be and what will come?
Will darkness or light be born?

What did it mean? Once again she longed for Trout. He was so much better at this stuff than she was.

Think about English classes, she told herself. Work it out.

Okay. The luminous, looping scrawl . . . that was the picture, the ultrasound. She could see exactly what Lou meant—the arc of the cranium, and the s-shaped curve of the spine were like a doctor's illegible handwriting. The dull opening was a part of the picture where the baby's skull (*her* skull) was in shadow. And apart from the bright white smear of her cheekbone and the small hollows of light that signified ear, eye, and spine, the rest of the picture, outside and in, was darkness.

So the poem was asking, what will be born? A baby of light? Or a girl made of darkness? *Am I evil?* Undine had asked Prospero. Is that what Lou meant? Will good or evil be born?

The back screen door slammed shut and Undine jumped. She slipped out of the room. Grunt was in the hallway. She tried to look less *slippy* and more like she was meant to be there, though her heart hammered her ribs. *Darkness*, she thought. *Light*.

Grunt gave her a peculiar look, or rather a look that told her she was peculiar. "Your dad's putting the boat away."

Undine didn't know anything about boats. Were boats put away? Apparently so. She'd had some idea they just bobbed about in the water all the time. She smiled stupidly and tried not to notice how good Grunt looked in his wetsuit.

She folded the poem surreptitiously behind her back and tucked it into her jacket pocket.

Grunt went into the bathroom to change. Undine busied herself making drinks.

She had hoped Richard might come today. She could have done with it—the physical, immediate distraction of Richard. She wanted him to look at her and say . . . oh, some movie thing about *only* and *always* and *can't stop*. He hadn't been so very cold in the car, had he? She could almost allow herself to believe this. Just embarrassed maybe, embarrassed by Lou walking in on them.

Or scared? Of her. *Will darkness or light be born?* He should have been scared. She *had* verged on darkness with him; she had almost controlled him completely. Prospero had said there were no witches or magic wands, no abracadabra, but one thing was for sure, Richard had been under her spell. Had Richard known it? Had he felt the darkness? Had Lou?

Grunt reappeared, and hung his wetsuit out to dry on the veranda. They took their drinks under the peppercorn tree. Grunt told her enthusiastically about the ship, the *Babylon*: "It's awesome. Your dad says no one's ever dived it. I'm going to try to get a team from the university. I couldn't do much today, I don't have my proper equipment, but the water's crystal clear and it's a pretty shallow site. She's still upright, though the masts are broken off. There's

242

plenty of bull kelp around, but it looks like we'll be able to work through that pretty easily. Prospero says it gets muddy after rain, and the silt on the bottom is loose, so I wouldn't want too many divers . . ."

Undine shivered, remembering her dream about the shipwreck. "Oh, it sounds so desolate."

"Poor *Babylon*," Grunt said. "Lying down there, her secrets submerged. Don't you think she deserves to have someone uncover them?"

Will darkness or light be born? What would Grunt find, hidden in that submarine forest of kelp? The bay had its own magic, Prospero had said so. Did magic sink ships?

She looked up and Grunt was watching her. She felt exposed, as though the poem were a glittering thread she wore for him to see.

"Is Richard working today?"

Grunt shrugged.

Undine raised her eyebrows and leaned back, inviting Grunt to speak.

Grunt sighed. "Just . . . don't expect too much from Richard, that's all."

"Why's that?" she asked coolly.

Grunt drew a circle in the dirt with his heel. "Richard's my friend and all, but I sure wouldn't want to be in love with him."

Undine almost laughed. "What's that supposed to mean?"

"Remember Lucy?"

The girl from the pub. The hair-flicker. So cozy with Richard, Undine knew there had been something between them. Some old spark. Not so old, she guessed. She closed her eyes, embarrassed for herself. It all made sense. Richard wasn't *scared* of her. He was two-timing her.

"Is he worth it?" Grunt asked, looking at her face.

"Is he worth what?"

"Stuffing up your relationship with your best friend?"

It struck her as unnecessarily cruel that Grunt should broach this subject when she couldn't broach it herself. It *had* seemed worth it when Richard was there, when he kissed her, or even just stood close, and she felt his warm breath on her skin. But away from him, it was different. She missed Trout.

"You must think I'm awful. Just like Dan."

"Dan?" Grunt sounded genuinely surprised. "Dan doesn't . . ."

"Yes, he does! At the pub, Dan was angry with both of us. Richard said . . ."

"Oh." Grunt's voice remained even and smooth. "Richard said."

"Just leave. Nobody asked you to come here. Leave me alone."

Deep down Undine knew she was angry at Richard, but as the anger rose up to the surface it somehow became twisted and confused. It sparked. She was alight with it.

"Undine . . ." Grunt tried, but she was on her feet. They stood there, staring at each other, Undine half wild, Grunt aware and wary.

She could feel the physical effects of the magic

work its way through her body. She knew what was happening. It was taking hold of her physical self.

"Go. Go. I said go." She heard desperation in her voice. I can't control it, she thought and a wave of dizziness and nausea nearly knocked her off her feet.

Power welled inside her. She didn't want to fight it. She wanted to destroy something. It was sudden and compelling. It was violent. She felt it surge through her arm, traveling through bone, blood, vessel, and skin. At the very last moment, she forced her hand away from Grunt, to protect him, and aimed instead at the peppercorn tree.

And then, the tree was gone. She felt a fierce exuberance at this awesome example of her power, Grunt forgotten. She was throwing off the ordinary, the mundane. Like before, with the storm, language left her. Nouns were weak, thin, and insubstantial. Verbs and adjectives hung useless in the air. She let them go, she threw them to the four corners of the garden.

Grunt opened his mouth to speak, but instead

he gasped dry air like a beached fish. He reached for her, grabbed her shoulder, appalled.

For a moment, still wild with the magic, she almost hurt him. She almost wanted to. She struggled, and he watched her struggle. Almost, the magic burst from her, almost she allowed it to, but she saw fear in Grunt's face and something else, something . . . She pulled tightly on the magic, she yanked it in hard like a lassoed beast and then—

The world was quiet again. Undine deflated. The magic slid away, out from under her, and she wobbled on her feet and was just herself again—still and ordinary.

Elated, exhausted, her body twitching with left-over adrenaline, she met Grunt's gaze, expecting fear—*wanting* him to be afraid. But he didn't look frightened. He didn't even look angry. He looked disgusted. He walked to the car, let himself in, and fired the engine. Without looking back, he drove away, skidding dangerously on the dirt road.

Undine was left in his wake, inhaling mouthfuls of dust and petrol fumes. As she walked up to the house she saw Grunt's wetsuit, still hanging over the veranda railing: empty, limp, waiting.

Prospero was in the kitchen, making egg sandwiches.

He didn't ask her about the peppercorn tree, and she did not tell him, though she knew *he* knew.

"Did I hear a car?" Prospero asked.

"Grunt . . . Alastair just left."

Prospero took a hard-boiled egg and tapped it on the bench, then rolled it under his hand until the whole egg was covered in a map of fine cracks. He began peeling it.

"Did you two have a fight?" he asked.

"No." Undine shivered. The magic had left her cold and numb. She remembered. "Oh. Yes."

"Well, you'll make it up. Isn't that the best part?"

Undine stared at him blankly, then realized what he meant. "Oh, Grunt . . . Alastair isn't my boyfriend."

Prospero winked. "Does he know that?"

"I have a boyfriend," she said, blankly. What had Grunt told her about Richard? The memory felt as distant as a cold, dead star. She didn't even care. "Or had. Richard. He's a friend of Alastair's."

"Is that the boy you call Trout?"

"No. Richard is Trout's older brother."

It all sounded so sordid as she tried to explain. It seemed so irrelevant too. She thought about the hot, fast presence of the magic. Her body ached from it . . . or for it. She realized with a start that she was already looking forward to the next time.

Prospero sat down at the table with a mortar and pestle, grinding seeds, chilies, oil, and lemon juice into a paste. "Remember I told you about this magic you possess?"

Undine barked a dry, humorless laugh. "The magic that possesses me."

"Yes, well. However you want to think of it. But be sure that it's a very attractive thing. Most people you meet won't understand it, nor will they guess at its true nature. But they will hear it resonating inside you, like a kind of electricity. People will be drawn to it. To you."

"So now you're saying," Undine said, quietly fuming, "that boys will only like me because of magic?"

"Not at all." Prospero ignored the barely muted hostility in Undine's voice. "Any man with sense will like you because you are beautiful, intelligent, and possess many other fine qualities. But there will be those who are drawn to you for empty reasons, and you will need to learn how to make the distinction. It is no different than if you were of exceptional beauty or if you were very wealthy."

"Oh crap," Undine said, tiredly. "That sucks."

Prospero smiled. "Some people would give anything to have this power of attraction."

"Not me. I'm not very good at relationships."

"A family curse, I'm afraid." Prospero laughed at the suddenly eager expression on Undine's face. "I'm speaking metaphorically. There's no actual curse."

Undine slumped down in her chair. "It would

have been a lot easier to blame all my problems on a curse."

"Indeed," Prospero agreed, and began mashing the eggs with a fork, adding the paste he had made.

They sat companionably in the kitchen, Prospero industrious while Undine stared out the window, thinking about, not Richard or even Trout, but Grunt, wondering if he had been drawn to the hum of magic inside her. Well, she thought, even if he had, the roar of it had driven him away. She doubted she would see him again.

The afternoon light dappled through the trees on the rivulet's walking track behind Trout's house. Trout aimlessly followed his feet, watched his shoes scuffing along the path. He couldn't get Undine out of his mind.

Behind the primary school he stopped where three boys crouched by the side of the rivulet, launching gumleaf boats. The boys ran along the rivulet to watch them race and Trout followed them, his long legs carrying him up the path on the water's edge. The vessels sailed splendidly until they hit a hidden eddy. Overcome, they spun wildly and then sank below the water's surface and were lost.

Not for the first time that day, Trout thought of Max and squirmed uneasily. Trout was still having second thoughts about having confided in Max. He'd felt safe at first, protected by the anonymity of the Internet. Or had he *wanted* to feel safe, because he had wanted information about Undine? To help her? Protect her? That's what he'd told himself. But deep down, Trout knew that his motives were less pure. He was driven, at least in part, by desire. Not just his feelings for Undine, but a scientist's passion for knowledge. And in attempting to satisfy that desire, he had put Undine at risk.

It wasn't Max he was scared of, not specifically. It was more . . . what? A world that knew about Undine. Worse, a world that could track her, locate her. Trout now realized that Undine's magic was the biggest secret both he and Undine would ever have. No one else could know about it.

The boys launched a new set of gumleaf boats from the same spot as before. This time only two of them drowned. Valiantly, the third struggled, submerged, and surfaced again. It pulled free and continued on the current. The boys followed its progress, pushing themselves through the long reedy grass on the bank of the rivulet, but Trout turned on the soft toe of his sandshoe and headed for home.

Outside, Undine inspected the site of the peppercorn tree. She found to her surprise that it was not gone, that she hadn't obliterated it entirely. Instead, in its place, planted unhappily in the ground, was a long and lumpy, largish frog, struggling to free itself. She dug the dirt away from around its elegant webbed toes which spread like roots in the soil. She tried not to touch it; it disgusted her a little, though it was not ugly, merely freakish.

A feathery cluster of leaves sprouted from a couple of bony protuberances on its back, as though the transformation was not quite complete.

Why a frog? she wondered. It was like something from a dream, strange and unlikely, but it still made sense, in a weird kind of way. Perhaps the magic came from the place where dreams come from, and spoke with its own coherent language. Or perhaps it was simply random.

The frog struggled free of the earth and sprang away, jumping rather comically over the ground and then disappearing into the bushy scrub that bordered the garden. It was disquieting to Undine that it should now be out in the world, free to breed with native frogs or be discovered by a curious eight-year-old frog-collector or even eaten by a kookaburra. But by the time Undine thought to catch it, or, she thought uneasily, kill it, the frog was gone, well camouflaged in the bracken and ferns of the forest's understory.

She looked up and thought she saw Prospero at

the kitchen window. She shielded her eyes from the sun and stepped closer. But there was no one there, just the beaded cord from the window shade, swinging to and fro.

CHAPTER TWENTY-TWO

Undine, who had always had a mother and no father, felt as if she were becoming a girl with a father and no mother—her Lou was becoming a distant thing, transparent and insubstantial. The past Lou, the one who had lived here with Prospero, was a stranger to Undine, yet she overshadowed the relatively ordinary Lou who had been Undine's mother up until now.

Undine herself was changing, as surely as the peppercorn tree had changed. The magic was a metamorphosis and as Lou was becoming less her mother, Undine was becoming less and less Lou's daughter.

Lying in bed thinking about this, Undine remembered the poem. Where was it? She'd tucked it in the pocket of her jacket, which she'd left in the living room.

The house was still, dim, and quiet, and she moved stealthily down the hallway. Prospero's door was closed. The curtains in the living room were open and the moonlight shone in, casting an unearthly greenish glow. She crept over to retrieve her jacket from the couch where she had left it.

The stillness was broken by a scream.

Undine dropped her jacket in fright and whirled around. A second scream cut the night air, and this time Undine realized it was coming from the bird's cage.

"Shut up," she hissed, but this only riled the bird more. He bobbed fretfully and swore profusely.

Undine fled back to her room.

Prospero's room was still quiet and dark, but now the door was ajar.

As she passed, Undine had the creeping sensation that he was there, watching her.

The dial-up tone rang through the modem. Trout clicked the link to the Chaosphere and opened up his own log-in details. In his hurry to sign up the other day, he had left nearly every heading blank, so the only thing other members could know about him was his username.

He located the button to cancel his membership, and hovered over it with the cursor, his finger resting lightly on the mousepad. For a moment he was almost tempted to stay. This was the only place he found he could explore Undine's magic, begin to understand it. He felt suddenly consumed by his scientific curiosity. Max had seemed smart; Trout could learn a lot from him. Maybe together they could . . .

No, he thought. That was exactly what he was afraid of for Undine. Knowledge was a powerful and dangerous thing. If anyone found out about Undine she wouldn't be safe.

He clicked the button and waited. The faint drone of the computer, and the eerie blue light of the screen in the otherwise dark silent house, were starting to freak Trout out a bit. The screen flashed up a confirmation message.

At the same time, a faint pinging noise emanated from the computer, quiet but unexpected enough to make Trout jump. Down in the bottom right corner next to the computer's clock, a little icon started flashing. It was the warning system for the antivirus software. It happened all the time, but tonight it scared the hell out of Trout. He didn't think to disconnect from the Web, or start the computer's shutdown sequence. He leaned over and unplugged the computer. The screen went black and Trout was plunged into darkness.

Undine dreamed of Richard.

She could smell his hair and the soil under his

fingertips; taste salt on his lips. They were kissing. She wanted it. Her hands were tangled in his hair. Shampoo and spice. She kissed his mouth hard, and her own mouth felt bruised and swollen, as if stung.

He gasped and she realized that as she kissed him she was drawing his breath from him, dragging oxygen up from his lungs. But she couldn't stop and neither could he, even when his ribs collapsed. She kissed him and his chest buckled and he gasped and choked and kissed her and his body twitched like a landed fish and then he was quite, quite still.

In a trance, Undine leaned over and inserted her fingers into his mouth, pulling it open. Leaning forward and speaking right into his mouth she whispered in a voice that was not her own: *"Will darkness or light be born?"*

In the tent he shared with Grunt, Richard twitched violently. Grunt woke up to the sound of Richard's breath, gasping and labored. It quickened and he began to wheeze, heaving in great mouthfuls of air, yet choking it out as if the mechanisms in his throat and lungs that permitted the passage of air were somehow faulty.

Grunt leaned over and shook Richard, shook him to wake him, but Richard twitched again and then lay distressingly still.

Grunt panicked and shook him harder, trying to shake the breath back into him.

"Richard!" he shouted. "Richard!"

And Richard coughed, breathed, keeled over, and slept: tranquil and ordinary.

In her dream, Undine pulled back, and it was not Richard who lay there, still, quiet, gray, dead. It was Trout.

Trout woke, his lungs seized up like a fist. He wheezed, trying to exhale.

He reached for the inhaler he kept by the bed, but it wasn't there. He panicked, fumbling to switch on his bedside lamp, which teetered perilously and fell with a crash to the floor.

The dream was still fresh, resonating like a clear bell in his mind. He could taste the salt water of Undine's mouth. He could even *smell* the dream: a mixed hazy scent of Undine, Richard's spicy aftershave, and something else, a faint waft of the sea. And he could hear that voice, not Undine's but as if a stranger were speaking through her.

He squeezed the air out of his lungs and gasped it in. His heart raced.

The overhead light came on, and his mother stood over him. She handed him his inhaler and sat on the chair beside his bed, waiting as Trout shook it with a rattle and breathed in the Ventolin.

"Again," his mother said.

Trout frowned. "I know," he tried to say, but he couldn't speak.

"Don't try to speak," his mother said.

Sometimes Trout suspected she liked him better during an attack, when she could say what she liked and he couldn't answer back.

"All right?"

Trout nodded. His breathing was much easier. He used the puffer again.

Mrs. M picked up the fallen lamp. "No damage done," she said cheerfully.

She kissed him, and pulled the duvet up under his chin, as if he were a small child. She switched off the light and closed the door quietly behind her.

Trout lay awake in the dark.

CHAPTER TWENTY-THREE

Undine woke suddenly. The magic from the day before had wiped her out. She still felt heavy from the aftereffects: limbs leaden, bones weak. The faint rosy light of predawn filtered through the diaphanous curtains. She rolled over and closed her eyes but she knew she wouldn't sleep again.

She thought about her dream. Richard. Did she even care, really, that he was not hers? She had known him for years in a peripheral sort of way. It had only been the last few days that he had been anything other than Trout's older brother. She had wanted him. She had wanted him to want her. But deep down, there was nothing. She was numb.

In the hallway she tried to keep her step light. But she needn't have bothered. Prospero was in the kitchen, spreading toast with butter as yellow as dandelions. "We've about quarter of an hour before the sun rises," he told her cheerfully.

"Oh."

"You did want to see the angels?"

"Mmm."

Undine chewed on a thick crust of sourdough toast.

In the garden Prospero pointed to the blank space where the tree had been. "What did you do to my peppercorn tree?" he grumbled, but she could hear joy and pride overflowing in his voice.

"Um," said Undine flatly, still tired and wrung out from her dream-filled sleep, "I turned it into a frog."

Prospero laughed. Perhaps he thought she was joking.

As they walked over the spot where the tree had been, Undine heard, and felt, some of the buzz of the magic, residual in the air. She remembered with a rush the power, the *magnitude* of it. How dangerous could she be? How dangerous did she *want* to be? And what, she whispered to herself, did she have to lose? Hadn't she already lost everything? Richard. Lou. Mim. Trout. Grunt. Had she lost herself? Had Undine, the girl of light, gone? Was Undine, the girl of darkness, her real, true self? She was so muddled by it all, she couldn't think clearly.

They walked down the beach path together. The air was still and cold. Undine took deep breaths of it. The sky was beginning to lighten the tufty, grassy dunes. Undine's father stopped just before the path dropped down to the beach.

"This is the best spot to see the sun rise. We'll wait here. We can walk out after, if you'd like."

At low tide the beach looked quite different. The half-moon shape was punctuated by jagged rocks at either end that, still wet, glistened blackly in the early morning light. They looked like teeth.

The sunrise, when it came, was amazing. At first it was just a point of light in the sky, growing, until a large round globe hung suspended over the horizon. The orange light from the sun hit the reddish brown rocks, and their haloes glowed pink, living every bit up to their names. She tried to relax, to be lulled by the beauty of it.

"Your mother loved it down here."

Undine looked quickly at Prospero. "Really?"

He nodded and smiled at her. "Oh yes. We used to come down here every morning when she was pregnant with you and swim in the sea. I loved to watch her, floating on her back, this huge buoyant belly bobbing up out of the water."

Undine wanted very badly to believe in a time when Lou and Prospero had been in love. It was like a safety net. No. It was like she was making a *deal* with herself . . . if Lou loved Prospero then she was born of love, of light. It was an unreliable shred of a thought. She tried to hang on to it, but the magic buzzed and droned and she found she couldn't concentrate on anything with the noise of the sea inside her.

"Shall we walk out?" Undine asked.

"Come on then." Prospero offered his hand and she took it.

Again, Undine was struck by an unexpected impression of youthfulness in Prospero. He seemed to be visibly younger. His left eye, which had been almost dead in its socket only two days before, now moved about with ease. His features were smoother, his face less worn. His body was suppler and strong.

The flashes of youth that had appeared before in him had passed quickly. This time, however, the youthfulness lingered.

Hand in hand they walked out toward the angels.

Trout was sick of jumping at every small noise. Bravely he had checked the computer. The antivirus software had done its job, and there was no sign in the stats that the attack had been anything more . . . *sinister* than usual.

But his dream was as present to him as his breakfast—he could taste it with every mouthful. He knew Undine was becoming lost. If he didn't find her soon, it might be too late.

He watched his mother and Dan leave with Mr. M. Dan jangled the car keys, ready for a driving lesson; Trout's mother twittered nervously. It was her day with Grandma, which made her edgy at the best of times. Certain doom with Dan at the wheel did nothing to improve her mood. Trout didn't mean to, but he found himself practically pushing them out the door.

"All right, already!" said Dan, annoyed.

"Quite," said Mrs. M. "What are you boys trying to do, drive me to an early grave?"

"No pun intended," grinned Dan, waving the car keys.

"Ha ha," said Trout, and shut the door behind them.

As soon as he heard the car engine start, and stall, and start again, he picked up the phone. He found his mother's address book and flicked through it, till his fingers settled on Grunt's mobile number.

"Hello?"

Trout didn't even identify himself. Fear for Undine made him bold. "Where is she?"

"Is this Trout?"

"I have to find her." Clipped, precise movie dialogue, no wasted words.

"Are you home by yourself?"

"Yep."

"When's your mum due back?"

"Not for hours."

"Good," said Grunt. "Wait there. I'm coming to get you."

When the doorbell rang, Trout was swift to answer it. But it wasn't Grunt; it was Lou and Jasper. The boy was clutching a fistful of colored markers.

"Jasper's going to sit nicely and draw while we talk. Is that okay?"

"I'm going to sit nicely," Jasper agreed. Trout suspected he'd been coached on the way.

"Um, yeah," said Trout, glancing at the clock. "That's fine."

He got Jasper some paper and settled him at the coffee table while he and Lou sat on the squishy leather sofa. From experience he knew to perch on the edge. Lou sat back and almost disappeared into the leather's luxurious folds. She pulled herself out and sat nervously as Trout sat, poised as if for flight.

"Trout, I came to apologize for the other day. I frightened you."

Trout was reluctant to admit he'd been frightened.

Lou went on. "It's just . . . I *must* know where she is."

"What about . . . what about Undine's father?"

"He died before she was born," Lou said, but her heart wasn't in it. She was reciting, like an amateur actor who knew her part but couldn't get into the role. She shook her head. "Undine believes he's dead. She always has." Despite her brave tone, Trout detected a faltering note.

"But he's not, is he? How could you?" Trout

blurted out. "How could you tell Undine her father is dead?"

Lou's eyes glittered and narrowed with anger, but then she shook herself, and it was as if her face were a white sheet and she was shaking out the creases, for after, her face was placid and carefully neutral.

"Is he dangerous? Is she in danger?"

Lou hesitated, and Trout wondered if she planned to keep telling her lie. For a moment he wondered if Lou thought that by sticking so steadfastly to her story she could will Undine safely home. But—out of sympathy for Trout, perhaps, or maybe to reassure herself by saying the words out loud—she said finally, "He won't hurt her, if that's what you mean. I doubt he could, even if he wanted to. But is he dangerous?" Lou shrugged. "It depends what you mean by dangerous."

They were interrupted by Jasper. He was still sitting, drawing, apparently oblivious to Trout and Lou's conversation. He held up his picture: wobbly circles inside wobbly circles.

"I'm drawing a picture for Undine," he said cheer-fully. "She's going swimming."

Trout felt a twinge of sadness for Jasper. "He doesn't know she's missing?" he asked Lou in a low voice.

"I tried to explain," she said hopelessly. "But that was what he thought I was saying. He has this idea that she's having a lovely time at the beach. It seemed cruel to keep insisting anything else."

Jasper said, "Aren't I sitting nicely?"

Trout nodded weakly as Lou stood up and began to pace around the room.

"So, I knew it. Well I didn't *know* it. I didn't want to believe . . . but part of me knew. Prospero."

Trout raised his eyebrows. "Like *The Tempest*? That's why he . . ."

"What?" Lou asked sharply.

"I think he's been . . . communicating with her."

Lou smiled, thin-lipped. "I'll bet he has."

They were circling around the topic of magic; nei-ther was prepared to say it out loud. Trout wondered how much Lou knew. She was certainly behaving strangely. On the one hand she had been to see him twice now, anxious in her search for Undine, who had, he pointed out to himself, only been gone a day and a night. Not even a full day. And yet Lou hadn't called the police, or gone looking for the less-than-dead father she had been lying about all these years. What was she so afraid of? What did she think she might find? Was it Prospero or Undine herself that Lou feared?

Trout believed Lou was genuinely concerned for Undine, but he still wasn't entirely sure he trusted her. After all, telling her daughter that her father was dead when he wasn't was a pretty awful thing to do in anybody's book. And there was that *thing*, that part of her he was sure he detected, a sneaky, private part, which maybe didn't care about Undine at all.

He sat watching Jasper fit more circles inside circles, and tried distractedly to think of an excuse to make Lou leave. But when Grunt rang the doorbell, Lou was still there.

Trout answered the door and went outside to talk to Grunt. Trout was shy of Grunt. He always felt childish and awkward around his brothers' friends, especially ones like Grunt: fit, healthy, active—all the things Trout wasn't.

"We can't go straightaway," he told him. "Lou, Undine's mum, is inside."

"She must be worried sick," Grunt said, and started in through the door. Trout grabbed his arm.

"Well, yeah. . . . But I don't think we should tell her where Undine is. Not yet, anyway."

"So she doesn't know, then? About Undine?"

"What do you mean?"

Grunt looked hard at him. "You know. You know what she is, what she can do. I can see it in your face."

God, Undine, Trout shouted at her in his head. Did you put out a press release yet? Don't you know how much danger you could be in? Is there anyone who doesn't know?

"So Richard knows too?" Trout asked bitterly.

"Richard hasn't seen her. Remember Lucy?" Trout nodded. Richard and Lucy had been on again, off again since high school. "Well, guess who's on the archaeology dig."

"On again?"

Grunt nodded grimly.

Back inside the house, Trout made the introductions quickly, using Grunt's real name, hoping Lou wouldn't recall that it was Grunt's mobile that Mrs. M had rung to track down Richard. She didn't seem to, though she looked intently at Grunt for a prolonged moment.

Jasper said, "Did you go swimming?"

Grunt smiled. "Not today."

Jasper showed him his drawing. "I'm drawing pictures for Undine."

"Are you, mate?" He leaned carefully over Jasper's shoulder and studied the drawing. Trout watched his eyes flicker, as though Grunt was seeing something extra in the drawing that Trout couldn't see. "That's a really good drawing. I bet

Undine would like it very much."

Jasper gave it to him. "You can give it to Undine, if you like," he said.

Grunt laughed nervously. "Yes," he said, winking at Lou to make it seem as if he was playing along. "Of course I'll give it to her. If I see her."

Lou smiled, without meaning it.

Grunt looked again at the drawing in his hand.

Trout said, "Lou, I don't mean to be rude, but Alastair's here to give me a lift to . . ." Trout was not a good liar. He could not think of anything off the top of his head and, panicked, he looked at Grunt, who was still examining the picture in his hand, oblivious to Trout's discomfort.

"Of course," Lou said easily, letting Trout off the hook. "Ring me, won't you, if you hear anything?"

"Yes," Trout said uncomfortably.

Jasper gathered up his markers. "Bye, Trout," he said. "Bye, Grunt."

After they'd left, Grunt murmured, "That's weird."

"What's weird?" Trout asked, picking up his house key and leaving a suitably vague note for his mother.

"That kid. You introduced me as Alastair. So how did he know that my nickname is Grunt?"

CHAPTER TWENTY-FOUR

Prospero nodded at the sea.

"Look at it," he said. "The power of it. The unruly drama of it. The weight."

The waves were over a meter high.

"It's amazing," agreed Undine, and she confessed: "I think . . . I think it's *in* me."

Prospero took two giant, bouncing steps into the water, steps that should have been impossible for his aged body. "I'm in the sea and the sea's in me!" he cried joyfully, hands raised above his head.

Undine laughed despite herself. She felt energy rushing through her again.

Suddenly Prospero was back on the beach beside her and he whispered beguilingly in her ear, "You know what would be fun? Test it. Be in it. Be in the sea. Let it sing, Undine. Undine Marine."

Undine hesitated. The newly risen sun was warm on her back. The sea shouted and roared, but underneath it whispered and hummed. She thought she knew what Prospero was asking her to do. He had said that the Bay had magic of its own, and her own magic that had been dormant for so long had accelerated with such velocity since she'd come here. Swimming here, in this sea, in the Bay where magic lived, who knew what might happen to her? But it called her. She wanted it.

She wanted to be annihilated by the waves, to be reborn into something wholly magical, into something that bore no consequences. For just a moment, she wanted that.

• • •

Grunt drove as fast as he could within the speed limit. Trout was surprised at how the Fiat flew.

"Why are you helping me?" Trout asked Grunt.

"She's in trouble."

"Her father . . . ?"

"Prospero?" Grunt tipped his head for a moment, thinking. "I dunno. He seemed all right to me."

"But Undine?"

"She's not handling it."

Trout didn't know how to put it into words. "The . . . the . . . ?"

"Yep." Grunt was quiet for a minute. "I don't think I've seen that much in my life. You know? Pretty sheltered existence. I knew there would be things out there, out in the world, things that would shake me up. Challenge my beliefs. But I never thought . . . I mean, how can she do those things?"

"It's pretty unbelievable, isn't it?"

"What's unbelievable is that I believe it. Like, it's just . . . Yep. It happens. Stuff happens."

Trout looked out the window. They drove past a

dead seagull; it lay intact and serene by the side of the road.

"Stuff happens," Trout agreed. "Stuff sure happens."

A moment was long enough.

Before she could change her mind, Undine waded in up to her waist, the undertow dragging at her clothes. She turned to look at Prospero, who was eager but also something else. Afraid, she thought. He's afraid. Of me. Her throat seized up and suddenly she was afraid of herself.

She turned around, desperate now to reverse her choice. She struggled against the undertow, but a wave struck her from behind and forced her down. The sea swallowed her whole.

Under the water she was confused. She swam what she thought was upward until she struck the unyielding sea floor. She panicked as the force of the undertow made the water churn around her. She resisted the chaos, pushing, pushing, wearing herself out, still unable to break through the surface of the sea.

She swallowed water, the strong brine burning her throat, and she began to cough, still submerged. Her chest spasmed, and by instinct she inhaled, and choked.

Undine felt as if she were free-falling. Or as if she were a spent wave, now part of the undertow, being pulled out to sea. Part of the Bay. She was Undine and yet she was not. She was who she would be if she had no need of skin, flesh. It was a surprisingly pleasurable sensation.

Huge swathes of kelp grew from the seabed. The light glinted green through the weeds. Fish schooled around her, rosy pink and silver. A shark with a cold eye silently pursued them.

Here the world was slow and functioned not by wit or thought but by instinct and survival. She began to understand the nature of the magic—not intellectual, or emotional, but composed of the same base elements. It was fueled by its own will to survive. It was animal, primal and instinctual. Blind, dumb, soundless, lethal.

The sea rushed through her.

She was the sea, she was Undine. Undine Marine, of the waves.

She disappeared, she vanished. For a moment she was truly and completely gone.

She reappeared.

She was born.

After what seemed like a lifetime, Undine crashed upward through the water's surface. She gasped, coughing and spluttering. She swam toward the shore, exhausted but desperate to get back to land. Finally her feet touched the bottom, and she was able to drag herself, walking, through the water and onto the sand.

Just before she collapsed she saw circles: wobbly circles inside wobbly circles, expanding from one central point into a giant circumference on the sand.

Behind her eyes, Undine started to spin. She sat up and was overcome by dizziness. She knew Prospero was talking to her, but she couldn't understand a thing he was saying.

"The circles," she said crossly. "What do they mean?"

She didn't hear Prospero's reply. She collapsed again, and lay, pallid and still, as if she were dead.

Undine came to in her room. She had no memory of how she came to be there.

She became aware that someone was with her. She couldn't see clearly, but it was a man, standing against the bright window, so she could only make out his silhouette. Tall, light-footed, sturdy, and spry, like the long, lean, flexing branch of a young tree.

Feeling defenseless, she pulled herself up, her head still reeling. She blinked, trying to clear her mind, her vision bleary from looking straight out the window into the brightness of the day.

The young man turned around. It was Prospero.

CHAPTER TWENTY-FIVE

There was no shifting now, no gradual transformation. This wasn't a trick of the light, an illusion. He was a much younger man. Had he appeared like this when Undine first met him she would have assumed he was younger than Lou. He came closer and she could see his face clearly. It was like being in the company of a stranger.

She pulled away, frightened by the change in him.

"You passed out on the beach. Do you remember?" he said.

"You're so young!"

"Do you know what it's like to grow old? To feel yourself *diminishing* day by day? To feel your spine coiling and your bones turn brittle?" His voice was rising to a high squeal. "To be old and forgotten, and splintered from the world?" He struggled to soften his voice—to soothe her, to beguile. "It's you, Undine. Your magic. You're doing this."

"No," said Undine. "This isn't me. I can feel it. It's different, like it's being pulled out of me. It's my magic, but I'm not doing it."

"This place," Prospero continued desperately, as if Undine hadn't spoken, "it's old too. Old and worn out with sadness. Shipwrecks. Hearts wrecked. It wants to go, to finish and be finished with. It's been forgotten so long, it just wants to disappear, to break off and become an island, a place that can't be left or traveled to. . . ."

"No," said Undine, reaching out with her mind, searching the magic around her, remembering what it was like when she was in the sea, when she fleetingly understood her power. "It's not the Bay that's doing this. . . ."

"Help me—help me tear a chunk off the world. Just the Bay. No one will miss it. . . . I'll give you everything," Prospero pleaded. "*Immortality.* You could have the world, you could nestle it in the palm of your hand. You could make a whole cosmos spiral out of an empty shell." He squeezed her wrist for emphasis.

But he was *too* desperate. Realization was dawning on Undine. "It's not yours to give," she said, marveling at this new idea. "It's mine. All the magic, all the power. You're using it, but it's mine."

"No," said Prospero, and she could hear a hint of his old, weak self coming from this younger body. "I called you. Magic attracts magic. This is your true home."

"You didn't call me," Undine said, working it out. "Not you. It was the Bay. The fish. The seaweed smell. You didn't send it. It was the Bay calling me. You don't have any magic. Somehow you have access to my magic, but you're just . . . you're a *leech*, a parasite."

Prospero seized Undine's fine, light hands in his large ones, clenching both her hands and his into fists. They burned where he pinched the skin, and she felt as if her bones might splinter in his crushing grasp.

It was a battle and the magic was the prize. He pulled and slashed and ripped and tore at it. She pulled back, tried to control it, but she couldn't. She couldn't find a way to shut him out.

His hands gripped hers tighter and tighter; her wrists were going to twist right off.

"Okay," she said finally, slumping her shoulders. "Okay. Don't squeeze so hard."

Prospero relaxed his grip and Undine took her chance.

"You're not strong," she said. "You're weak. You're weak." And she wrenched herself from his grasp.

When she ran, she ran to the sea. The sea had changed her, she had been stronger there. She needed to get back to it, to reclaim her magic from Prospero. It was a risk, because Prospero knew the sea, knew how to draw magic from it. That must have been how he had gained access to Undine's magic in the first place. This is why Prospero had wanted her, she thought, choking back a dry, angry sob. He didn't *love* her. He didn't want a daughter. He simply wanted her power, to possess her magic. Well, she wasn't going to let him have it. It was hers and she would protect it. Instinct. Survival.

The tide was coming in. She stood with the sea up to her knees. It was instant, the rush, the power she felt. It was like being in the eye of the storm. A storm, that was something she knew about. She was the eye. She saw everything.

In the garden the lemon tree shivered slightly, as if stung by a cold breeze. The roses swayed and the grass began to roll and swell crazily.

Around the boundaries of the garden, Undine made a storm. It was nothing like the cloudburst she'd created in Hobart. That was merely a pale shadow of a storm. Surrounding the garden now was a squalling wall of wind, pounding the air. It was like being inside a cyclone. Standing on the beach, she could see the same wall of wind hauling up a barrier of water. In this way she began to seal off the bay, creating a boundary that Prospero could not cross. By the time she sealed him up inside she would be gone, far out to sea.

When they pulled up in front of the house, Grunt and Trout were unable to fathom what they saw. They sat in the car, speechless, staring at the wild wall of weather.

Grunt shook himself. "We have to find Undine," he said. He pushed open the door, only to have it almost ripped off the car by the force of the wind generated by the event occurring in the Bay. The sound was unbearably loud. Both Trout and Grunt automatically covered their ears.

Trout was sickened. He had witnessed that first event, that other storm, but it had meant nothing to him. It was just science—chaos, disorder, and patterns of order emerging from disorder. But this . . . This was powerful and strange. This was dangerous, deadly. This belonged outside science. He was scared for Undine, and suddenly, he was scared *of* Undine.

"What has she done?" he gasped. He turned to Grunt, who was ready to launch himself through the wall.

"No! We don't know what's going to happen to us in there!" Trout yelled.

"There's only one way to find out," Grunt shouted back. "I'll take the house. You check the beach. We have to find her!"

Trout ran toward the water, punching his body through the wind, stumbling often, falling once, and hauling himself back onto his feet. He found his way to the path and down to the beach, where the wind died down, and he was able to straighten up and run normally. He half jogged, half ran, shouting out her name: "Undine! Undine!"

There she was, thigh-deep in the water, her red hair distinctive against the wash of sea and sky.

"Undine!" he screamed. "Undine!"

He ran out into the water, jumping and waving, desperately trying to get her attention.

She turned. He hardly recognized her. She was changing constantly; seasons passed through her and whole planets formed and died in her eyes.

"No, Trout! Go back! Go away. You don't belong here!"

"Undine? What's going on? What are you doing?" He couldn't keep the horror out of his voice. "Stop, for god's sake."

"What would you know? What would you know about anything?" And then she looked at him again. "You're scared of me," she said, and she laughed.

Trout could hardly see in this creature the girl he knew. She was changing into something half-ocean.

"Undine," he said softly. "What happened to you?" He reached out to touch her.

"I grew strong," she answered. "You're weak."

And she plunged into the water, striking out against the powerful current.

"Undine!" His voice cracked. He pulled off his shoes, threw them back in the direction of the beach, and ran deep enough to dive into the water.

Trout was no athlete; nevertheless he'd done swimming for his asthma since he was very small and was a capable swimmer. Grim and determined, he swam toward her, concentrating on powerful, even strokes and keeping his breathing steady.

He didn't see the wave coming. It struck him, and it felt as if he had been hit by a wall of rock. Momentarily he was aware of a strange pulling sensation, the water rushing noisily around his head; then there was silence—bitter, cold silence—and everything went black.

Grunt felt the air trying to tear him to pieces as he hauled himself toward the house. Wind whipped his eyes until they wept. He pushed on, but lost his bearings, unable to see the house through the squall. He stopped, struggling to orient himself. Wind rushed around him. He found himself caught up in the tunnel of air. Darkness descended over his already sore, struggling eyes. Just before the world went black he saw . . . Prospero?

"Get out of here!" the young Prospero called. And then, as if he had seen something Grunt couldn't see, "Oh my god. You idiots! What did you think you could do? Who's going to save you?" He howled, "You fools. This was my chance. This was *my* time."

Grunt felt an overwhelming *pull*, as if he were being wrenched into pieces, and then suddenly the awful noise stopped and he was struck by utter silence.

Am I dead?

Small sounds began to reassert themselves on the world—the whirr of a cricket, a bird's song, and the far-off hum of a car approaching. His vision cleared and the blackness began to dissolve into light.

He was on the long tarmac highway, far up the coast. Alone, adrift by the side of the road.

• • •

"Trout!"

Undine watched in horror as Trout went under. *What have I done? What have I done?* She waited, frozen. But he didn't reappear.

She swam, desperate and panicky. She lost her bearings, and couldn't remember exactly where she had seen him submerge.

"Trout," she was sobbing. "Trout. Trout."

She dived, searching with her hands; her eyes were open but only just able to make out shapes under the water. She no longer felt powerful. She felt weak, her limbs as soft and flaccid as noodles. The salt water scratched at her throat and eyes. The magic seemed to flow out of her, emptying into the sea. She surfaced, forced air into her lungs, and dived again.

She felt him first, the slipperiness of his skin under the water. She heaved him upward to the surface, and then surfaced herself, struggling to drag air into her sore lungs.

Trout was limp in the water, his head twisted,

facing away from her. He was not conscious, but he was breathing. She held him with one arm and swam with the other, kicking back toward the beach.

The magic was gone. The magic was nothing. Her muscles ached. She was desperately tired but she pushed herself. The water stung her eyes. Her nose and throat were sore from the salt.

"Okay." She was talking more to comfort herself than Trout. "I'm going to get you to the beach. And then you're going to be okay. You're going to be just fine. We just have to get to the beach. We just have to get to the beach and everything will be fine."

Undine believed it. While they were in the water Trout was in danger. But as soon as they were on land, he would be fine.

Towing Trout slowed her down considerably, and it took her what seemed like hours but was actually only minutes to get back to the shore. She reached a place where she could stand and began pulling him out. At first it was easy, as he was weightless in the water, but then it became almost impossible. Using all her strength, she was able to drag him onto the firm sand just above the waterline.

He twitched, then was still.

"Okay," she gasped. "Okay. You're going to be fine. You have to be." She bent down to him and listened for his breathing. Nothing. She felt desperately for a pulse.

His heart had stopped beating.

"Oh no," she sobbed. "Oh my god."

Trout was dead.

CHAPTER TWENTY-SIX

Undine screamed. Time stretched and folded and shuddered inside that scream.

She seized the magic that she'd released into the sea. It ebbed and flowed around her. She gathered it up and gave herself to it completely. She grew enormous and dangerous. The Bay became a fleck, a grain, a speck. She gathered the sky around her and set the earth spinning on its end.

She screamed, to break the world in two.

• • •

"Undine!"

It was Prospero. He stood before her, enormous like her. She looked into his rejuvenated face. He seemed to be shifting before her very eyes, changing with the landscape, duplicitous and unreliable.

But she was changing too. She could feel her different parts within collide, fracture, and pull away, like the movement of continents.

Wind rolled around the Bay. The sea leaped up in fury, immense waves smashing against the sand.

"Undine!" he shouted. Magic flickered around his young face, his body. But it was nothing compared to the magic she possessed. He was a pale candle and she stood poised to puff him out.

"Isn't this what you wanted?" she said, and there was a deafening rip. Undine realized that the Bay itself was literally being torn from the world. "You began it. I'm ending it."

"Undine," he implored. "You have to stop it. You'll kill us both."

"So?"

The Bay shook. The angels began to crumble, turning to dust and falling into the sea.

"What does it matter? Who cares if we die?"

The sky ruptured, leaking black through the atmosphere.

Prospero cowered. She hated him. He was weak. She felt strong.

"Who cares if *you* die? An old man, out here on your own. No one ever visits. A daughter you've never once called, in sixteen years."

The ground rolled underneath them. Above them, the sky continued to ooze a thick liquid black. The blackness spread down toward the sea. It surrounded them until the only light was a small but rapidly declining orb around Prospero and Undine.

"Undine," begged Prospero, who seemed to be having trouble breathing. "Undine, please, make it stop."

"I will. Make it. It will all. Just. Stop."

"Undine. Please, I want you to—"

"To what?"

"—to live."

Her head dropped. The hard red fiery stone of anger inside her melted away. She felt numb with grief. But she wanted to live too. Despite it all. The loss, the hardness of life, the flintiness. She wanted to live.

She could no longer see Prospero. The Bay had been all but overcome by darkness. One tiny pinprick of light the size of a grain of sand flickered.

"End it," she told Prospero, wearily. "Finish it."

"I can't," said Prospero. "It has to be you."

Her bones ached. "I don't know how."

"Yes. You do."

"But what's left? Is the world even there?"

"I don't know," answered Prospero. "Is it?"

And then from somewhere close she heard another voice. It was soft, warm, curved, female. It asked, tenderly, *Will darkness or light be born?* and then answered itself:

Light. Light.

Undine fixed her tired eyes on the grain of light. It blurred in and out of focus and almost vanished.

She saw what that grain of light was made of. It was the rivulet, where she had sat with Trout a lifetime ago. It was making daisy chains with Fran on the hill above the school oval. It was swinging upside down on the monkey bars. It was a slice of watermelon in summer, crisp and ice-cold against her teeth. It was the first night after Stephen had died, lying between stiff clean sheets, listening to herself cry in the dark. It was the scarlet sunset the night Jasper was born, and Lou and Undine singing "Molly Malone" between contractions. It was Jasper's vegemite smile. It was the first bite of an apple and the last bite of Mim's fabulous chocolate cake.

"End it," said Prospero, gently.

Undine ended it. The Bay tilted, slid, exploded in a bright burst of white. And everything was restored, regular and ordinary. Undine looked up.

Standing on the path, at the zenith of the dunes that formed the boundary between the beach and the garden, a last haze of magic framing her like sunlight, emanating from her—soft, warm, curved, female—was Lou.

CHAPTER TWENTY-SEVEN

That hug. The warmth of Lou seeping in. Undine closed her eyes. She wanted to reside there forever. Prospero hung back.

Undine couldn't speak. Her voice was as heavy as lead, weighed down somewhere deep in her diaphragm, and she couldn't bring it to the surface. The magic wasn't gone. It was still there, inside her, but dormant, and safely contained.

In her heart she cried for Trout. She led Lou down to the beach to find him. Prospero followed.

It took Lou to say it, but as soon as she did, Undine could see it was true: "That's not Trout."

It was a close approximation. But the hue of his skin, the shape of his face . . . they were not quite right.

"End it," said Lou. "It has to be you."

Undine shot Lou a nervous glance. "I don't know if I can."

Lou took her by both hands. "Undine, listen to me. The magic, it doesn't have to be like that. You're strong. You can control it."

But Undine was still afraid. She turned to Prospero. "Can't you do it?" she asked him.

Lou answered for him. "This is *your* magic. *You* have to end it." Her voice was gentle. "I'm right here," she added.

Undine laid her hands on the lifeless husk of almost-Trout. She could feel his body emptying of magic, could feel it drawing back up into her. It pumped through her like blood, and she felt the rush of power returning. Momentarily she felt the adrenaline, the threat of it, but she held it tight, thinking about that seed of light.

Lou whispered, "Remember, you can control it." Undine focused. Though she drew the heady magic out of the body beneath her hands and into herself, so that it coursed through her blood and muscle and bone, she managed to push it down into her most secret self, where it would have to live for now.

Under her hands, the packaging of skin and flesh that had been Trout was transforming into something else. It shrank to something smaller and smoother. It grew scales and fins and a blank gaping eye.

Lou and Undine stared down at the slender, dead fish that lay on the sand where Trout had lain. It stared back at them, but the eye was dead and the body was still.

"Prospero," hissed Lou, venom and loathing stinging her voice.

But Undine knew. "Not Prospero. I wanted to find Trout so badly, I *made* him. Trout wasn't there to be found. Was he?"

Lou shook her head. "No, sweetheart. He's up at

the car. I found him on the side of the road."

"Is he . . . ?"

"He's fine."

Undine looked at the fish. "I killed it. When I brought it out of the water, it died."

They sat together in silence, mourning the death of the blameless fish.

Behind them, Prospero grieved too.

"Prospero," said Lou. "You're looking *old*."

Undine lifted her head and looked at Prospero, and he *was* looking old. The magic had drained out of him too. Undine felt almost sorry for him. He looked down and Undine saw shame and fear on his face.

"What have you done to my daughter?"

"She's mine too," said Prospero, sounding like a belligerent child. "She's mine. I wanted her."

"You wanted her? When did you ever want her? You wanted her magic. Just like you wanted mine."

"Yours?" whispered Undine. "Yours. I never even thought of you."

Lou nodded. "You think you got magic like that from *him*?"

"I was here. I was always here." Prospero's voice was plaintive and the shakiness had returned. "Everybody had forgotten me."

Undine felt a twinge of grief for him.

"You didn't care," said Lou. "This was the way you wanted it. You never wanted to be a father. You just wanted her to emerge fully grown."

"You told me he was dead," Undine reminded her.

"Oh, Undine," Lou said. "I was protecting you."

"But he's still my father."

Lou put her hand on Undine's face. "He didn't want a little baby. He wanted you, as you are now. He wanted your power. He wanted mine."

"Why didn't you tell me about the magic?"

"I hoped I wouldn't have to. I hoped I was . . . unique. And in the last week, well, I could feel the magic in you, the strength of it. It frightened me. I knew I had to talk to you about it, but it was like you were becoming . . . less mine. More of an adult, I suppose. I didn't know whether to hold on or let go. In the end I did both, and neither."

Prospero rocked like a pendulum, and Undine jumped forward to catch him before he fell. "Come on," she said to her mother. "We have to get him up to the house."

Lou hung back, as if reluctant to touch him.

"Come on," insisted Undine.

They steered him toward the house, the three of them leaning on each other. Undine wondered briefly what it might have been like if they had been a family.

"But who pulled Trout out of the Bay?" Undine wondered. "Was it you?" she asked Lou.

"No," said Lou.

They both looked at Prospero.

He said nothing.

Trout and Jasper were leaning on Lou's yellow station wagon. Undine dropped Prospero's arm and ran to Trout. She punched him, quite hard (he rubbed his shoulder vigorously and looked vexed), and then she collapsed on him. He caught her but was almost knocked over by the sheer force of her, so they did what looked like a very clumsy dance around Trout's large feet.

Trout pushed her away gently. "Stop crying all over me," he half joked. But it was his way of saying he was not ready to forgive her.

"What happened to you?"

Trout shrugged. "I don't know. One minute I was swimming toward you, and then there was that monster wave. I felt . . . something kind of *snatch* me. All of a sudden I was sitting on the edge of the peninsula road, my clothes soaking wet. Anyway, I think I might have passed out, because then Lou was standing over me, and she put me in the car and here we are."

"How much do you remember? From . . . before that?"

"Enough," Trout said, and wouldn't meet her eye.

"I'm sorry," she whispered. She looked at him. "I'm

so sorry. I want to hug you." But she didn't. He kept his arms stiffly beside him.

"I'll get over it," Trout said.

Undine's mouth twitched downward.

"Look," said Trout. "I really will get over it. Just not for a while. Besides"—he gave her a shove—"I still haven't forgiven you for kissing Richard." She caught him midshove. It was all right. It would be.

Jasper tickled her side. "Hello, bruvver," Undine said, and gave him a squeaky kiss.

"Here comes Grunt," Jasper said.

Undine realized that the Fiat was parked in front of Lou's car. But Grunt was walking from the opposite direction, down the dirt road.

"Forgot my wetsuit," he said laconically.

"Right," said Undine.

"You okay?"

Undine nodded. "You?"

Grunt smiled.

The four of them walked back toward the house.

• • •

Trout, in the solitude of his bedroom late at night when he had put away his textbooks and his scientific calculator and turned off his bedside lamp, had often imagined what it would be like to rescue Undine.

In his mind, it would be Undine who was drowning, or threatened by sinister assailants or attacked by wild dogs. Trout would be the hero, the one who pulled her from the water or fought off her attackers. In his fantasies the rescued Undine would turn breathlessly to face him and suddenly realize how much she loved and desired him. In the light of day, he had always felt a bit ashamed of how masculine and sexist his fantasies were. But now he was not sure who was the rescued and who the rescuer. Who was the assailant, and who the assailed?

It was a strangely surreal and yet almost idyllic scene. Prospero sat, solitary and rigid, on the veranda, where Lou had deposited him. Trout and Undine sat together—it was as if Undine was reluctant to let living, breathing Trout too far from her side. Grunt, a small distance away, was being assailed equally by Jasper and

Ariel the woolly dog. Lou stood planted in the garden, surveying plants that had once been her own.

Undine watched Lou with an attentive, even quizzical expression, as if she was seeing Lou for the first time after a long, long absence. Trout watched Undine. Trout smiled. His heart ached. His heart aching, that was in the smile. He didn't mean for it to be, but somehow it crept in. Undine smiled ruefully back and looked away again.

It frustrated Trout that to Undine he was an open book and she could skip to the last page. He didn't want it to be this way; he wanted to hold something back, so he had something to reveal later when she, rescued and breathless, looked up into his eyes.

"It's never going to happen," he told himself firmly, but old habits are hard to break and he only half believed it.

"What are you mumbling?" Undine asked.

"Oh . . ." Trout was caught off guard. "You know. Shakespeare."

Undine smiled. "Yeah, right. You are so weird."

"What now?" Trout asked her. "The magic? What are you going to do with it?"

"I was thinking about it," Undine said dreamily, because she knew she had plenty of time to decide. Lou had kept her magic hidden for all these years—concealed even from her own daughter. So it was possible to keep it pushed down, safe and *tidy*, where no one would see it. But to Undine it seemed kind of wrong too, to turn her back completely on her magic. Yes it was frightening and hard to control, and yet she admitted to herself, she was still intrigued by it, by its immense possibilities. "What if I studied the weather? Learned about weather systems? Then I could use it, learn to use it. To help people. I could bring rain and calm oceans." She laughed self-consciously.

Trout smiled sadly. It was a nice idea. But ecosystems are so complex, so fragile. What could happen? A butterfly flaps its wings in Japan . . . He could see no place for Undine's magic in the natural world.

He remembered Max, and the Chaosphere. He knew now that Undine's magic hadn't been his secret to tell. He *had* put her at risk; his instinct to quit the Web site had been right. He still felt that pull, that scientific urge to dissect the magic, to analyze its parts. So Trout would still get to protect Undine. He would rescue her a little bit every day, from his own desire, and she would never thank him for it.

Undine was looking at him again. She took his fingers in her hand, and this time he didn't pull away from her. The warmth of her fingers seeped right through him, turning his bones to liquid.

"Undine," he began, and then stopped, because the very second he started he knew how ridiculous the words would sound. And once they had been committed to air, they would live forever in the space between them, eventually forming something terrible and insurmountable, and their friendship would be lost to it.

Undine smiled gratefully, because he had stopped. "You know I love you," she said, apologetically.

Trout smiled weakly. Because it wasn't enough, and they both knew it.

CHAPTER TWENTY-EIGHT

Inside, Jasper had discovered Caliban, much to the little boy's delight and the bird's disgust.

"Budgie!" Jasper said gleefully.

If birds had eyebrows, Caliban would have raised his.

"You're not exposing my child to that inside-out feather cushion are you?" Lou called. Caliban shrieked.

"Get plucked, birdbrain," said Trout, and Jasper squealed with laughter.

Undine looked up to see that Grunt was watching

her. She had avoided being alone with him all after-noon, her feelings conflicted. They stood for a moment, considering each other. Undine went out-side to catch her breath.

She was worried about what Prospero had said, about men finding the magic inside her attractive. She didn't want to trick Grunt as she had Richard—poor, hopeless, two-timing Richard—into falling in love with her. She imagined him hypnotized, like a cartoon on TV, a zombie with his arms outstretched.

Though Grunt had seemed immune to it. Perhaps somewhere inside him he even despised her a little. From the look of disgust on his face when he'd driven away, she'd been sure that he hated her. But he'd come back. Did he like her? She just couldn't tell.

Trout was the only one she could be sure of—she *knew* his feelings for her were more than just the zing of the magic. She sighed. The irony was that she didn't want Trout.

She sat down on the veranda step. Perhaps she wasn't ready for love. And yet it had started now.

First Richard, now Grunt. There was no putting it away for later. She wondered if Lou had ever felt this way about Prospero.

Something caught her eye, distracting her from her train of thought. Underneath the boards of the veranda there was a barely perceptible movement. Undine peered between the slats.

It was the cat of the other day, but she was no longer pregnant. Instead, heaped together so one could barely be told from another, were three—no, four—kittens. They were odd-looking things, not at all catty yet, but long and seal-like, with tiny ears pressed flat against their heads.

She went inside to get Jasper, to show him the kittens, but found Prospero lurking unhappily in the hallway, and brought him outside instead.

"Look," she said, pointing. "Kittens."

"Humph."

"Whose cat is this anyway?" Undine asked him.

"Nobody's cat. A stray. I've seen her before."

"Well, she's your cat now," Undine stated firmly.

"She's chosen you. And you have four new kittens."

Prospero mumbled something about being more of a dog person.

"Piffle," Undine dismissed him. "It will do you good to have some helpless things to love. And everyone loves kittens. Who couldn't?"

Prospero said gruffly, "There are too many people in the house. I'm taking Ariel for a walk."

Undine said, "I'll come with you."

Prospero did not argue, but called Ariel and set off down the path, Undine beside him.

She thought she might actually learn to love Prospero. It was like some tired, aching muscle deep inside her: it needed exercising, but it *was* there, it had made itself known to her now.

As they walked down the path, Undine asked, "Do you really mind them all being here? You seemed to . . . I don't know. Enjoy my company. I thought you liked having me around."

"Everything's changing," Prospero complained. "It's all different. For years this place barely existed."

"And you. You barely existed with it."

"Barely."

"Is that why you never tried to see me?"

Prospero smiled. "I knew you would come. You've been the thing that has kept me alive. Kept me existing."

"Yes, but in Normal Land people ring on the phone. It might have been nice to have a father."

Prospero shrugged. "You didn't miss me."

"I missed you. I just didn't know what I was missing."

"What did I have to offer? I'm no good at families."

"I could have decided that. Besides," Undine went on shyly, "I think you have been good at it these past few days. There were times when you shone."

"Really?"

Undine nodded.

Despite himself, Prospero looked pleased.

"So," Undine went on, "then it's a good thing? You know, that I didn't destroy us both and obliterate the universe?"

"I wanted to be young again. Strong and powerful.

I wanted to feel the magic pouring through me."

"But it was *so* wrong," Undine said. "Don't you see? I *want* to grow up. I want to get old. I want to watch Jasper grow up. I want to fall in love. Get married maybe. Have a baby one day. Even if it means getting sick and dying. To stay a teenager forever . . ." Undine shuddered. "Look, I'm kind of hoping life gets better than this. I want to make it past twenty so I can find out."

Prospero grunted. "I suppose I want those things for you too. When you were just the idea of you, the hum of magic in the air, well, it didn't matter. But the fact of you. That's a different story."

"I gave up the magic. When I thought Trout was dead, I gave it away into the sea. You could have taken it all, couldn't you?"

Prospero closed his eyes, as if he suddenly couldn't bear to look at all that blue. He nodded.

"But you used it to pull Trout out of the Bay instead. And Grunt too. You protected them."

He opened his eyes. "No. I protected you. You

could never have survived hurting them. I'm just a selfish old man, Undine. I just wanted to keep you whole. It was my loss that I was worried about. The loss of you."

Undine smiled.

As Grunt, Trout, Jasper, and Lou appeared over the rise, Ariel stood at the shore barking happily at them.

"I guess she'll never be much of a watchdog," Prospero said gloomily. "She never had to be before."

"That's good too," Undine said firmly. "She'll be a welcoming dog. It will do you good to have visitors."

Prospero grumbled softly to himself.

"Here you are," said Lou. "You've been gone for ages."

Jasper took Undine's hand.

"This is where you went swimming," Jasper said.

"Yes! I did go swimming here." She picked him up and buried her face in his stomach, blowing raspberries. "What a clever boy you are to know that."

Jasper squealed and wriggled free. He knelt down

and patted the sand. "And this is where I did my drawings."

"What?" Undine asked, attentive. "What drawings?"

Jasper ran up to Grunt and asked him something. Grunt, remembering, pulled a folded piece of paper from his pocket and gave it to Jasper.

With great care, Jasper opened it out flat and smoothed away the creases before running back to Undine. "Here," he said, handing her the paper. "I did this for you when you were gone away."

On the page were circles inside circles, wonky, crooked, but gorgeous. She recognized them immediately.

"Thank you," Undine said, and she hugged Jasper tightly. "Thank you, gorgeous boy." She folded the drawing again and put it carefully in her pocket.

"Come on," Lou said. "Home. You've got exams to study for, remember? And plenty of time to do it, seeing as you're grounded till you're twenty-four."

• • •

When they left, Prospero tried not to look too relieved to see them all go.

"Now," Undine bossed. "I'm going to phone you as soon as I get back. And I expect a letter about the kittens, telling me how they're all doing. You'd better go to the shops and buy some cat food. And you have to name them. You can write that in the letter too. And no *Tempest* names. Ordinary ones, like Mittens and Polly."

"And look after my garden," Lou said. "The lemon tree wants feeding."

Jasper said, "Good-bye, Mr. Man. Thanks for the sandwiches."

Grunt left first. As he said good-bye, his fingers brushed Undine's so lightly that she wasn't even sure if it was intentional.

The light was getting long and late. Shadows reached across the road, though behind them the day still glittered brightly. As they wound around the snaking highway, Undine caught the occasional glimpse of the indigo sea.

Trout sat behind Lou in the station wagon, watching Undine's face. He thought of *The Tempest*, of Miranda's brave new world. He wondered how Miranda had navigated this new world, after the play had ended. He thought of how heartless Shakespeare had been, to leave her there, unaided, unobserved. But then, that was life, wasn't it?

Undine opened the car window and tasted the wind. They overtook the Fiat. Undine waved. The Fiat puttered happily, eating their dust.

Out on the rumpled sheet of the sea, a yacht traveled northward, the sail tipping and bowing happily in the wind. Beyond the boat, there was the straight blue line of the horizon. A pale daytime moon hung over the water, slender and brittle as a fingernail.

And beyond the horizon, beyond the moon, who knew what lay there?

"*O brave,*" Undine said to the wind, "*new world.*"